Daddy Issues

Written by
Viv Love

Printed in the United States of America.
ISBN: 978-0-9982706-1-6
First Printing, 2016
Val Pugh Publishing
www.valpughlove.com
Shreveport, LA 71129

Acknowledgments

Of course, I must thank **God** first. Without Him, there would be no me. I thank Him for my talent, confidence, dedication, family, friends, and supporters.

Thanks to my **husband and best friend, Willie**. You have always supported my dreams and made my life easier. I appreciate the millions of times you allowed me to read to you. I thank you for sincerely being interested in my story. Thanks for your ideas, support, and love. You are truly a blessing.

To my babies, **Chandler, Chase, Tre, and Kennedy**, thanks so much for believing in me and for thinking that your mom is awesome and famous. Thanks for being cool characters in my children's books. Your bravery helped me become more confident. Your talents helped me embrace mine. You are all so amazing, and I love you endlessly.

To my siblings **Kenya, De'Shima, Paulika, and Paul (LaTonya)**, thanks so much for your input when I texted you all hours of the day and night. I appreciate your honesty, support, and sincerity. Thank you for buying my books without expecting anything free. Your support and input means so much to me. When I am rich, I'll take you all on a nice vacation. ☺

Mom and Dad, thanks for your support and for always telling everyone what your baby girl is doing. Your love, support, and all the times you bragged on me helped me push even harder. I love you both so much...

Grandma (and Mama Annie), thanks for being the inspiration for my first book. You opened so many doors for me, and I will love you forever.

Cousins, Wolfpack, Elementary Friends, and Childhood Friends! You already know what it is. Thanks for your input, continued support, and for being eager to read this book. I hope I didn't disappoint you!

Aunts and Uncles, thanks for being proud of me. That helped fuel my passion.

Social Media family, the likes, shares, and comments really do help! You all made me feel famous lol. Thanks for your support. A special thanks for the heartfelt inboxes.

TBSP, thanks so much for your input, referrals, and support!

Editing clients, thanks for being brutally honest with me, just as I was with you. Watching each of you win awards and write multiple books helped fuel my drive. Keep up the great work!

Kanika, this cover is amazing! People do judge a book by its cover. Thank you for making my readers want to read my book. You stuck with the vision and gave me life!

This has not been an easy journey, but it has truly been worth the fight. I love you all!

Queen V

~

"I've got the stuff that you want.
I've got the thing that you need.
I've got more than enough
To make you drop to your knees.
'Cause I'm the queen of the night;
The queen of the night..."

Whitney Houston

~

Introduction

My name is Vivian McQueen, and I am a counselor by day and Queen the Dominatrix by night. Although my father died when I was a baby, I grew up hating him. From what I've heard, he was mean, horny, drunk, and abusive to my mother. I can believe that he would have hated me as much as I hate him. The stories of my father messed me up so bad mentally that I brought baggage into every relationship I ever attempted with a man. I expected them all to abuse me, cheat on me, hurt me, and make a fool of my love. I expected them to be my father.

In an effort to get over the pain of my issues, I began to search for a cure through excessive dating. I dated executives, firefighters, younger men, fat men, fine men, older men, and even drug dealers. Each date only fueled my resentment and daddy issues, because each man had the characteristics of my daddy. After so many years of failed relationships, Queen, my alter ego began to form inside me just as a fetus grows inside a woman's womb. I could feel her develop more each day, and I longed for the day she would be born. Her desires became my desires, and her behaviors began to take over me.

She was born on the day that the firefighter choked me during sex. I was afraid that he'd kill me, yet I had no desire to remove his hands from my neck. The more he choked me, the harder he fucked me. The harder he fucked me, the closer I came to climaxing. When I released my juices on his dick, Queen was born. Her birth changed my life completely. I became a different person, and my sexual appetite grew darker, while my sexual addiction grew stronger. I continued to date, and the failed attempts became less painful with my alter ego in control. Queen introduced me to a world that few people know exists. In her world, men are bound by chains, handcuffs, spikes, and whips. They refer to her as Queen or Madam, and they submit to her commands. The men are punished for causing pain, and they are forced to provide sexual pleasure to women as Queen sees fit. Not all of the submissives are willing participants, but that's their punishment for hurting innocent women. Besides, pain is the new pleasure...

Chapter 1
The Beginning

My mother, Bella McQueen, is a strikingly beautiful woman with creamy dark skin and light brown eyes. From the looks of her nice figure on a 5'6" frame, you'd think she was still a model instead of a recovering cocaine addict. Sadly, her life took a turn for the worst when she was raped by her stepfather. He was the only father that she knew, and she was always very close to him. I remember her telling me how they had such a perfect family at one point in time. Her parents would take her and her siblings to the aquarium in Baton Rouge every summer. They'd go to church together at least twice a month, and they always had family gatherings at their house. Everything was good until her stepfather lost his job and found a drinking habit. It started with a glass of wine here or there. He would dress up in the mornings and spend the day searching for a new job. After a long day of being rejected, he'd relax with a couple of drinks. When the wine couldn't erase his depression, he switched to bourbon and then scotch.

As her stepfather's drinking habits progressed, so did his dirty looks that eventually led to him forcing himself on my mother one drunken night. He promised to kill my grandmother, my mother, and my mother's siblings if she told anyone what happened. So, at the age of seventeen, my mom hopped on a bus and headed to Northwest Louisiana. She picked up a job as a stripper at the local gentlemen's club. One of her stripper friends helped her secure a fake I.D., and she jumped head first into the fast money lifestyle. When the tips weren't flowing fast enough, she would take on escort jobs.

One night, she got called on an escort gig that changed the game for good. When she showed up to meet with this particular client, she was surprised by how sexy he was. She entered the room prepared to do her job, collect her money, and wait for the next call. However, this client had the room laid out like some shit off TV. There were candles and rose petals everywhere. He had soft music playing and wine chilling. She could have sworn she was either in the wrong room or being punk'd. Her client was very polite when she entered the room. He offered her a glass of wine with a side of bright red fresh strawberries. He was a gorgeous man with thick, curly hair and intoxicating grey eyes. His skin tone was a beautiful golden hue, and his smile that was accompanied by one dimple in his left cheek could light up any room.

Bella accepted the wine, and they spent the rest of the evening getting to know each other. She eventually learned that her client purposely sought her out because he was captivated by her beauty. He informed her that he was interested in showing her a life of luxury. They sat and talked for a while, and she learned that his mother named him Vincent Bourdeaux, but he was known as Vinny or Daddy in the streets. Vinny had a rough childhood in the 9th Ward of New Orleans, so his mama moved him and his brother to Shreveport. His father was incarcerated for beating a man to death who tried to rob his mother. The cops also added a few drugs charges on him. Vincent had a hard time coping with his father being in jail. Therefore, that led him to selling drugs by the time he was eleven years old.

He was the kingpin of his area until he was busted and sentenced to juvenile life at the age of fourteen. That didn't stop his flow though. You see, he was a lil nigga with big balls. He was taking orders from his father who was still respected in the streets while he was locked up in Alcatraz. Vinny served his time in juvie and went right back to running the streets like his pops trained him. Although his mother moved him and his brother to Shreveport, he still made a name for himself in the streets. Nothing came through without his permission – no drugs, escorts, prostitutes, stolen goods, nothing.

He had been watching Bella for a while, and he knew that he had to have her. Like every other woman that crossed paths with Vinny, my mother became hooked on him like she was hooked on the pipe. After a night of ecstasy, he convinced her to leave the club and work for him full time.

He was willing to pay her double, but she had to abide by his rules. My mother became the main girl for the man who would become my brothers' father. He also happened to be the biggest pimp and drug dealer in the city. Although Vinny took good care of Bella, she gave birth to my two older brothers in a drug-infested motel in Bossier. He never involved the police or paramedics in any of his affairs. He had a few doctors, lawyers, politicians, and other officials on his payroll, so he would call them up as needed. His on-call doctor delivered both of my brothers.

After several years of working the streets and becoming more addicted to drugs, my mother decided to leave Vinny. When she broke the news that she was leaving, he kicked her ass, emptied her purse, and sent her on her way without my brothers. He even reminded her that she was only good for sucking, fucking, and making pretty babies. That's some shit to say to the woman who brought in over $5,000 each week.

Bella took on a job as a waitress at a local sports bar. She made good tips, but they didn't hold a flame to the money she made with Vinny. Eventually, she grew tired of the rude customers and chump change tips. However, since she wasn't familiar with Shreveport, she couldn't just jump back into the street life. Therefore, she began to canvas the city to see if the street life was worth living again.

She eventually met my father who was a high-functioning alcoholic and an occasional drug user. Based on the stories I heard growing up, their relationship started off really well just like any other relationship my mother had with a man. Then, things somehow turned sour, and my mom was left alone again. At a young age, I began to think that my mother was a punk who didn't know how to handle men. I really hate that she had such a terrible history with her relationships. She's far too beautiful and kind to have to deal with the disrespect she has faced.

***

I was born and raised in the early '80s in the MLK area of Shreveport, LA. We all know that every low-income black neighborhood has a street named after the hood's first black president - Dr. Martin Luther King, Jr. My mother did the best she could do for me. Vinny rarely let her see my brothers. She had a rocky life after my daddy beat her into labor while she was pregnant with me. Luckily, we both survived the brutal attacking. Too bad his ass died instantly when my mother shot him in the back of his head a month later. I wish the motherfucker had suffered brain damage instead of being lucky enough to die.

When I was a kid, I always asked my mom why I didn't have a dad like the other kids in school. She would always change the subject by asking me about my day. I remember seeing her eyes well up with tears each time, but she never answered my question. I was ten years old when I found out the truth about my daddy. My aunt came over to visit with my mother, and I had to go in my room as usual. I would always close my door and play with my toys until Aunt D.K. left, but something was different about the visit this time. Aunt D.K. brought a gold envelope that had my mother's name written on it. Mother looked petrified after she peeked at the envelope's contents. I didn't know what was in that envelope, but I was determined to find out.

As I sat in my room with a cup against the wall, I could hear my mother begin to cry. Aunt D.K. whispered that she would make it all disappear. I was anxious to know what *it* was that had my mom in such a panic. They turned on some music to drown out their voices, so I crept out of my bedroom into the hallway to hear them better. As I crawled down the hall, I could see my mother holding up a newspaper article that read: *Detectives Have a Lead in the Slaying of Franklin Camden.* I didn't know who Franklin Camden was, but something told me that my mother had something to do with his murder. The strange thing is that the man looked familiar to me, even though I'd never seen him a day in my life. I kept staring at his picture until it hit me, and I knew he had to be my daddy.

My mom and auntie were so wrapped up in their conversation that they didn't even realize that I was sitting behind the couch with my knees pulled up to my chest. I knew I was likely to get a good old-fashioned whoopin' for listening to grown folks' conversation, but I needed to know the truth about Franklin Camden. While I sat as still and as quietly as I could, my mother began to speak very calmly and quietly about *that night*.

"D.K., it wasn't planned. I swear it wasn't. I just didn't want him to hurt us again. Vivian had to stay in NICU for three months because of what that motherfucker did to me. I had been at the hospital all day long, and I just needed some fresh air. So I decided to go for a walk to clear my head. As I walked through the park, I could tell someone was following me. I turned around several times, but no one was there. I even dipped into the sandwich shop just to be sure I wasn't crazy.

"I sat for about ten minutes, and everything seemed normal. So I decided to head on back to the hospital. Suddenly, someone grabbed me and covered my mouth. The fumes from the cloth knocked me out, and I woke up inside Frankie C's apartment. My panties were soaked in blood, and he sat at the foot of the bed smoking a damn crack pipe. That son of a bitch raped me and popped my damn stitches. I guess he didn't expect me to wake up, because he sat with his back to me as he continued to get high. I managed to grab his gun from the nightstand without disturbing him. Apparently, he had plans to kill me, since his silencer was attached. Without a second thought, I shot that motherfucker in the back of his damn head.

"I was in so much pain, but I managed to change the sheets and remove the cover that was protecting the mattress from the blood that was pouring from my vagina. I changed into the clothes that I left at his place the last time I was there. I threw the bloody clothes and mattress cover in a big trash bag and disposed of them at the hospital. I knew it wouldn't be taboo if they found the bloody items there. I got back to the hospital just in time for the nurses to make their rounds. It was so busy in there that night, so no one even knew I had left. I didn't mean to do it, D.K.! I swear! That motherfucker was gonna kill me, and I wasn't having that. My baby girl needed me..."

"Keep your voice down, Bella," Aunt D.K. whispered. "I told you that I will take care of everything. You just take this money, and take my niece on a little trip. By the time you return, this will all be a dream."

Aunt D.K. handed my mother a stack of hundreds that totaled ten thousand dollars. My heart raced as I thought about everything I'd just heard. I didn't know what was going to happen next, but I eased to my room and began to pack my things. We were headed on a vacation thanks to my mother killing my abusive father. It didn't really matter much to me where we were going. I was just ready to leave the hood for a while. My mom walked Aunt D.K. outside. Meanwhile, I packed everything that could fit into my Rainbow Bright duffle bag, including my Cabbage Patch dolls. I didn't know where we were going, but I was going to be ready.

When my mother came back in, she came straight to my room. I could tell that she tried to fix her face up so I wouldn't know that she was crying, but her eyes were red and puffy. Still, she tried to perk up and act normal.

"Hey kiddo. What are you doing in here?" she asked as she sat on my twin bed and glanced at my packed bags.

"Oh, I'm just playing with my doll," I said, trying to act as if I didn't follow her eyes.

"You going somewhere?"

Knowing my cover was blown, I had to confess that I overheard her conversation with Aunt D.K.

"Well... um... I kinda heard you and Aunt D.K. talking, and I know we have to go out of town for a little bit. I just wanted to be ready so you wouldn't have to wait on me. I know it's an emergency, and I have your back, Mama."

"Baby girl, you know how I feel about you eavesdropping. I'm not gonna whip your butt this time, but make that your last time ever listening to my conversations. What all did you hear?"

"I think I know who my daddy is, and I know why he's never been around. Is it true, Mama? Did he really do those bad things to you? If he did, I'm glad you killed that nig-... I mean... I'm glad he wasn't around me! A man better never ever hurt me like that man did you! He ain't my daddy! I swear I'll punish any man that even thinks about hurting you, me, or any woman ever again!" I exclaimed as I grabbed my plastic orange baseball bat for protection from whomever.

"Calm down, macho-woman. I don't want you to worry about anything. Don't you breathe a word of this to your cousins. When you're a little

18

older, I'll tell you more. As of right now, make sure you have enough clothes for two weeks. We're going on a road trip. I figure we can visit your cousins in Dallas for a few days, and then fly on out to Oakland to see some more cousins."

Although I wanted more information about the horrible things that happened to my mother, I decided to drop the subject for a while. I hated to see my mom feeling sad or forcing herself to be strong. The pain in her eyes was accompanied by bags and dark circles from being tired. I could tell that she wanted to tell me everything, but I was just a little too young. In a way, I'm glad that the truth is different from what I imagined. Either way, I made up my young mind to always protect my mom and every woman I know from the horrible men in the world. In fact, I even planned to punish a man or two for my father's transgressions. It may have been wrong to feel that way, but I needed something to fill that void. Therapists might call it daddy issues, but I call it sweet revenge.

Chapter 2
Vivian

The city streets are full of noonday travelers who are either headed to lunch or to business meetings that will consume the rest of their afternoon. My day has flowed rather smoothly, so far. I've been able to catch up on progress notes, and I even got a chance to water the orchid I received from one of my clients. It was a small token of her appreciation for my services. After finishing all of the sessions that went along with her program plan, she was actually able to rekindle the flames in her marriage. She even got her husband to respect her more than ever before. You see, my marital counseling services are different from what couples usually receive. In fact, I don't even meet with the husbands at all. My sessions are for the women only, and my goal is to get them to figure out how to make their husbands treat them like royalty.

I actually used to be a traditional marriage counselor. However, after so many years of seeing my female clients hurt, abused, and disrespected, I decided to switch up my approach. In the traditional sessions, it was usually the women who set them up in the first place. Therefore, the men weren't very cooperative at all. They were obviously there to try to avoid paying spousal and child support. Meanwhile, their eyes and demeanors showed how much they were already gone from the marriage. Each couple was allotted fifteen sessions over a six-month period. For the successful marriages, I saw improvements by the fifth session. Although that was a rare occasion, fifteen percent of the marriages actually worked.

The other eighty-five percent of the marriages still had turmoil after the eighth session. What's even worse is that most of the men continued to cheat on their wives. If they weren't cheating, they were disrespecting the women by being rude, condescending, and uncooperative. The women would sometimes show up to the sessions without their husbands, because the men refused to keep trying. Rather than let their money go to waste, I would spend those last sessions trying to repair the broken women. We would discuss all of the complaints that the husbands had from weight to cooking and cleaning to sex. For each complaint, we would discuss ways to improve. Even if the marriages were dissolved, at least the women would be empowered, strong, confident, and dominant rather than weak, hurt divorcees.

Seeing the growth in those women and the unchanging hearts of their husbands encouraged me to change my counseling techniques. My current clients are loyal, female only, and under contract. As a result, they don't disclose the full scope of services. They simply refer other ladies to me for marriage counseling, and I do the rest. Since it's warm out, business has been booming lately with all the men still acting up. They usually behave better in the winter time with the holiday season and all. Once the weather warms up, so do their hormones. It never fails. They fuck up at home, and then their wives get word of my counseling services and come running.

Although my current caseload is rather full, I'm actually pretty much free for the rest of the day. It looks like I'll have time to go to the queendom before heading home. In fact, I'm probably going to go on and shut it down now and head out.

"Excuse me, Vivian. I have a woman here that's in desperate need of your platinum services. She's willing to pay in full today," Maria buzzes my phone as I'm gathering my belongings to leave the office.

"Did you explain the process to her?"

"Yes, ma'am... She knows how it works. She says she was referred by a previous client whose husband learned his lesson, thanks to Queen."

Is Maria really mentioning Queen over the intercom? Who the hell could this mystery person be? Furthermore, which one of those bitches will I have to tame for opening their mouths?

"Send her back, please."

Maria knows how discreet I am when it comes to Queen. If she's disclosing that much information, this better be good. While I'm mentally sorting through my client list to find the weakest link, the mystery shopper knocks lightly on the door. I shift nervously in my seat before greeting her. I've never been nervous meeting a client before, but I suddenly feel hot. I manage to tell her to come in, between the short breaths I'm taking. When the door opens, a tall, slim woman appears. She has a dark complexion, and she's sporting long dreads that reach halfway down her back. Her body is athletic, her smile is radiant and calming, and her eyes are intoxicating. I clear my throat before speaking.

"Ahem... Good afternoon. As you know, I'm Vivian McQueen. And, you are?"

The visitor extends her hand to shake mine. I notice that her nails are perfectly manicured, and there's a tan line where her wedding band once was. She gives me a slow, seductive once-over that makes me even more nervous than before. *What the fuck is it about this damn woman? I'm not attracted to her. Shit, I'm just really fucking nervous for some reason.*

"Hi Vivian. You can call me Mrs. Black for now."

"Okay, Mrs. Black. How may I help you?"

"You've helped me enough by providing this service to women who have been hurt. I've actually come here to help *you*."

"Help *me*? Well, I work independently. I'm not looking for a partner. However, if you'd like my counseling services, I need you to fill out this packet. Once it's completed, I'll be able to determine your level of need."

When I try to hand the packet to Mrs. Black, she turns her head and walks to my oversized bay window. As she stands in my favorite spot, gazing sixteen floors down at the busy streets on the corner of Spring Street and Fannin Street, I notice that she's rather tall. In fact, she's taller than the average woman. Her presence has really taken ownership in my office.

"You're welcome to have a seat, Mrs. Black. Would you care for a bottle of water?" I offer in an attempt to regain control of my office.

"Thanks, but I actually like this view much better," she replies.

Surprisingly, she accepts the bottle of water and takes a sip.

"Oh... kay... well... Who referred you to me? I'd love to send them a thank-you card."

While I await a response, Mrs. Black continues to peer down at the busy traffic. I can't help but feel like she has a familiarity about her. I need her to give me some type of clue to jog my memory. After a brief silence, she finally decides to speak.

"A thank-you card won't be necessary. I'll consider completing your little packet on my next visit. I have to run right now. My afternoon appointment awaits. I just wanted to meet you in person. Is this your card?" she asks, as she reaches for the stack of business cards on my desk.

"Yes. Please help yourself to one. When would you like for us to pencil you in for your appointment? We typically don't take walk-ins."

"I don't know just yet. I'll be sure to give you a buzz after I've checked my schedule. Tootles..." Mrs. Black says as she disappears through my office door.

Her perfume and presence have me torn between being mesmerized and trapped in a state of shock. Luckily, she left the half-empty bottle of water on the windowsill. I'll get Medgar to process her fingerprints immediately. I need to find out who the hell she is as soon as I can. I also need to know which one of my clients will be punished for breaching our confidentiality policy. There isn't one client on my roster who doesn't know about the Queendom. In the brochure, they see the beautiful spa, waterfalls, workout facilities, fine dining, and a beautiful mansion, and they immediately want to sign up. I take the time to explain the details of the mystery mansion, and I even offer them a tour before they choose their package. They sign their contract first, so I don't worry about them disclosing details of the Queendom. Even if they opt of Queen's platinum services, they are still subject to a private party if they break any of our rules.

My close friend, Medgar, owns a small private investigation firm a few blocks over on

Edwards Street. We have been working together for years. He used to conduct investigations for me when the wives felt like their husbands were cheating on them. He also checked the women out for me, too. I liked to know that I could fully trust every word my clients said. Sometimes, Medgar and I stretched the law a bit, so I just made him a regular on my payroll. My clients pay me really well. Therefore, I can take care of him with ease. His substantial salary also gives me the power to get my paperwork processed quickly. I need to drop this water bottle off to him immediately. I must know who Mrs. Black is and who sent her. It seems as though a lucky lady will be visiting the Queendom pretty soon.

Chapter 3

Cheyenne

Marissa and I have been co-owners of Xpressions Nail Spa for almost ten years. We met at cosmetology school back in 2006, and we've been tight ever since. We attended Red River Beauty School, and I graduated as the valedictorian. Marissa was the salutatorian. Since we both were top nail technicians in school, we spent a lot of time working together and training the newer students. I guess our business relationship was destined to happen. Since going into business together, everything has been virtually perfect between us. We have never had any financial issues, and our families have pretty much combined. If either of us are absent from work, we don't mind if the other one sees our clients. Our relationship is just cool like that.

Overall, my life is good. My love life is even picking up. Since I broke up with my crazy ex, I have been too scared and too busy to try to date anyone else. Marissa has been dating some mystery guy, so she hasn't had much time for girl talk. It's cool though, because I actually joined a dating site a couple of months ago.

About a week after I joined, a guy named TD&H began sweating me. I've communicated with him, and he seems really nice. We actually plan to meet this weekend. I just hope his screen name stands for Tall, Dark, & Handsome instead of Tired, Dirty, & Hurt. Furthermore, I pray that his appearance matches my hopes for his name. I usually don't go on blind dates, but I haven't had much luck with the guys I've seen. I figured I'd switch up my approach to see how that turns out.

My computer love and I have had great conversations for the past couple of months. His real name is Miguel. He lives in Chicago and works a lot. That's why he hasn't been able to make time to see me. He's finally going to be free this weekend, so he's flying to Louisiana to see me. We're meeting at a local restaurant. I wish Marissa could be in the restaurant during my date, but she won't be in town. She usually sits at a nearby table on first dates just in case something pops off. She's going to see her family in Tacoma, Washington this weekend for a reunion. She asked me to go with her, but I didn't want to miss a chance to meet my new boo.

Anyway, I'm forced to be a big girl and go on my date solo. I'm kind of anxious to meet him. I hope this fool isn't cross-eyed like the guy Ishmael that my aunt tried to push off on me. She claims she didn't know his eyes were messed up. I told her that she should have known something was wrong if his ass sat in church wearing shades every Sunday. I damn sure hope he doesn't stutter like Stanley, the cop that works as a security guard at my mom's school. I can imagine how his ass sounds trying to tell somebody why the hell he stopped them. Now, he could be sexy like Willie the artist that worked with my cousin. He could even be cute like Idris or fine like Ghost.

Regardless of his appearance, I don't plan to give up the nookie on the first date. However, I do need to schedule an appointment for a bikini wax just in case. Hell, it's been over six months, and I have needs. I can only use so many damn sex toys from the L.O.V.E. Adult Toy Line. I'm gonna fuck around and get electrocuted with all the damn electrical currents flowing through my bath water every night. I often imagine that I'm lying in the arms of my computer love as he rubs vigorously on my clit until I cum in the warm, lavender scented bath water.

Miguel is half-Dominican and half-Black, which is basically fully black with a bit of Hispanic in the mix. He says he works out at least four days a week, and he enjoys playing basketball. If all of this is true, I can't be sure that I'll be able to resist mounting him this weekend. Let's just hope his ass isn't catfishing me though. I've heard so many stories about big fat greasy ass dudes posting profile pictures of sexy men and pretending to be them. They woo the women with great personalities, and then they show up on dates in hopes that their inner beauty prevails. Well, call me shallow, but I need to at least *like* the outside beauty if I'm going to date somebody. I mean, I'm not perfect by any means, but I would like to be able to at least find the banana to insert it in my split. I can't be digging all through crevices for the treasure. I'm sorry, but that's just not my thing.

Miguel's profile picture is an image of the African flag. My profile picture is the outline of Africa with the black fist in the middle. That's what made him reach out to me. We share similar interests in our people and our culture. We agreed that we wouldn't exchange pictures until after we have seen each other. I didn't mind this because I'm not really looking for anything serious anyway. Even if he's not my type, we can still keep each other company with discussions of our African history. He's even teaching me some stuff about his Dominican side. If he's not crazy, I'm even willing to meet him in the Dominican Republic to explore the culture and taste the authentic food. I've had plantains here at a Dominican restaurant on the lake, and they weren't too bad. Miguel swears that his abuela is the best at cooking them.

When he gets here on Friday, we're going to meet at Sister's Seafood to give him a taste of some good ole Louisiana soul food. I've talked about the tartar sauce so much that he plans to take jar home with him. I recommend that he tries the stuffed shrimp, rice and gravy, and buttery toast. I don't know how the hell those women make toast so damn good, but I can eat it dipped in tartar sauce all day long. Hell, I hated rice and gravy until one of the older waitresses that has been with them since the beginning forced me to try theirs. Now, when I don't feel like cooking, I swing by and grab their special at least once a week.

After we finish eating, I'm going to show him how to play poker at one of the casinos in Bossier. He's never gambled before, but he's willing to learn. He hopes that beginner's luck will earn him some extra cash. I'll probably let him play around on 3-Card Poker for a while. I'm afraid of introducing him to the poker room. He might run into some millionaire that will bully the table and take his money. Most of the people who play in the poker room are regulars. They'll quickly realize that Miguel is a newcomer, and they'll likely handle him badly. I'm not trying to ruin his time here. We might skip the casino altogether and just chill at Jazzy's Lounge. He's from Chicago, so I'm sure he can swing dance. We can take over the dance floor with some smooth ass dipping and swaying while the band performs. If he can guide me on the dance floor, there's no telling what he can do in the bedroom.

That reminds me - I need to go on and schedule that appointment with Senoj for a full body waxing. She works in the shop with us, and she's a bad ass esthetician. We met in college, and I promised her a job when she got her license. Our relationship started out as business, but we quickly became friends. She works with Marissa and me part-time. She also works with her friends at their make-up bar and photography studio. Her friend, DeToya, is a celebrity make-up stylist, and the other one, DeShun, is professional photographer. They actually have a cool setup. That's why I don't mind her splitting her time between us.

My cousin Shirea owns a limo service. Since Marissa can't discreetly join me on my date. I can at least ask Shirea to have one of her guys to drive us around. That will at least lessen my chances of being kidnapped. I have too much to live for, and I'm not trying to die in an effort to find love. I know love hurts, but I damn sure don't need it to be fatal. Shirea has some heavy hitters on her team, so I'm sure she'll send one of the Cooper Road boys on this job.

Her homeboy, PJ, is very chill and handsome. He has a great smile, a thick beard, and he even wears braces. He dresses really nice and seems like a regular dude. What most people don't know is that he is as crazy as they come, and he's rumored to have a body or two floating in the Red River. If she sends him as my driver, Miguel's ass better not even sneeze wrong. Once I finish up at the shop, I'm going to call my girls to get everything lined up for the weekend. I'm looking forward to seeing what it will bring.

Chapter 4

Marissa

For some reason, I'm rather excited about seeing my family for a few days. It's been a while since I even attended a family reunion. With business picking up at the salon, I haven't had time to even think about the leaving the city. Now, I'm not complaining, though. More business means more money. More money means we can finally finish the renovations at the salon. Thanks to those needed renovations, I met the new love of my life. His name is Tyrone, and he is everything that I crave in a man and more! Luckily, Cheyenne wasn't able to join me to meet the contractors a few months ago. If she had been there, I'm sure Tyrone would have chosen her 5'9" athletic frame over my 5'5" thick frame. Don't get it twisted, I'm fine as wine, honey. However, some men prefer Cheyenne's long legs and chocolate skin over my sexy caramel self. I'm not hating, because neither of us have had the best luck with men. Therefore, her long legs saved me a few bumps and bruises along the way.

Unfortunately, Tyrone won't be able to join me on my trip. He has a huge contract with the city, and the rain has set them back a few days. I damn sure wanted to show him off to my boughetto ass cousins from L.A. They love to rent dates and brag about all of the movies they've been in or the red carpet affairs they've attended. I know there's no way that those bad-built bitches can land such successful men like that without either paying for them, sucking for them, or begging for some damn charity work. Anyway, I'll just pack my bottle of tequila, and let it be my date for the weekend.

Working with Cheyenne has been great over this ten-year span. She's become more like family than a business partner. Between our busy schedules and Tyrone's big contracts, I haven't gotten the chance to introduce them to each other. Tyrone is the sweetest man I've ever met, and Cheyenne is cool as a fan. I know she'll definitely approve of him for me. I mean, I don't need her approval to date, but she's like a sister to me, and her opinion really does matter. Maybe I can cook dinner when I return from my trip and invite them both over. Hopefully, we'll be able to synchronize our watches for a few hours. I'm sure Cheyenne will have a list of questions to ensure that Tyrone is good enough for me.

Tyrone and I have been dating for a couple of months, and I still don't know much about him. I've never been to his house before, but he's been to mine. We've had sex several times, but he never spends the night. He has to wake up really early to head to the construction sites, and he doesn't want to disturb my sleep. Therefore, he stays until I fall asleep, and then he lets himself out. He's always considerate of my time and feelings. He's very gentle, and a beast in the sheets. I feel my feelings growing for him, but I don't want to set myself up to be hurt again. I can get Cheyenne to ask him all of the questions that have been brewing in my mind.

Meanwhile, I'm just going to take it slowly and enjoy the moments with him. I miss him when he's not around for a few days. So I know this trip may be a little tough for me. Maybe I'll swing by the construction site before I head to the airport. I could use a few kisses on his smooth, soft, full lips. I love the way he nibbles on my bottom lip and sucks on my tongue each time we connect. To top off his sexiness, his long dreads always smell so good. I love the way he throws his head back to remove them from his face before he kisses me. Hell, on second thought, by the way my panties are getting wet, I may need to skip the kiss before I mess around and miss my damn flight. I'll just call him when I'm on my way to the airport.

Chapter 5

Vivian

My mystery shopper's strong presence left me feeling some type of way. So I decided to skip the queendom and head to the gym to release the tension. When my clients sign up for services with me, I ask them to provide me with a picture of them with their spouses. They think it's for me to see an image of happiness in their marriages. However, it's my way of finding out what their husbands look like so I can have Medgar keep an eye on them. Their behavior in the streets determines their punishment level with Queen. Some of the women are skeptical to release the photos, but I assure them that everything is confidential. Sometimes if they need a bit of extra persuading, Queen might come up behind them and reach down in their... purses to retrieve a picture. Needless to say, I know what all of my clients' husbands look like.

During my ride to the gym, I couldn't help but think about Mrs. Black's presence in my office. Something about her eyes made me feel like I've met her before. Unless she has a twin, I know that I know this lady from somewhere. I need Medgar to hurry up with those DNA results. He said that he'd process them instantly, but that's not even fast enough for me. Maybe I'll be more relaxed after my workout. In fact, since my gym is downtown, I'm going to park my car a few blocks away from the gym and jog there to get warmed up. The nice spring breeze is perfect for a run anyway. I just hope those construction workers are too busy to bother me today.

Once I parked my car, I quickly stretched my legs, turned on *Kem Radio* on Pandora, inserted my ear buds, and took off down Travis Street. There wasn't much traffic since lunch time was over. The sound of Kem singing *Love Calls* was already taking my mind to another place. It's just something about his sexy voice that removes all of my worries and stress. I've heard people complain that all of songs sound the same. However, it's just the uniqueness of his voice that makes you quickly realize who's singing. I don't think his songs sound the same. His voice is just unchanging, and it has soothed me countless times. Therefore, I'm a bit defensive if I hear anyone speak ill of Kem.

Apparently I was running a bit faster than a jog, because *Love Calls* wasn't even halfway through, and I was already approaching the construction site near Travis Street and Edwards Street. As much as I hated passing through that area, Kem had me feeling sexy, and the breeze was blowing through my long ponytail just right. I decided to humor the boys that day. A little fun never hurt anyone. Besides, Queen could definitely use another victim. I saw a tall dark one that looked like he needed to be tamed anyway. I slowed my jog down just a little bit to get a better look. His arms and complexion were a plus. I wondered what his hair was like under that hard hat.

Just as I got closer to the site, my target reached for his hat as if he was about to remove it. Suddenly, an older man in a white button down shirt approached, and my target dropped his hands to his sides. *Damn*, I thought to myself. I was so close to getting a better glimpse of my soon to be concubine. I assumed that was another contractor because the man was holding a clipboard, and he appeared to be requesting something from my victim. They finished the conversation, and the older man walked off. Although there was a nice breeze out, Louisiana weather brings a bit of heat with every season. This time, the heat worked in my favor, because my victim removed his hat. As soon as he did, I lost my footing and hit the ground! I couldn't believe my eyes!

I was staring at none other than Mrs. Black! Yes, Mrs. Black is a damn man! In fact, she or he or whatever... is the same damn man that whistled at me a couple of months ago when I was downtown. That's why his ass... her ass... whoever's ass looked so damn familiar to me this afternoon in my office! My instincts never lie. I can't wait to reach Medgar to find out more about this motherfucker. What kind of shit is this? What is this Mrs. Black up to? Whatever it is, I can't let him see me. I have to play it cool, despite the fact that I just crawled into this office building in the middle of the afternoon.

My damn ankle was killing me, but I needed to figure out how the hell I was gonna get out of that damn building without Black seeing me... I called Maria to come pick me up and take me to my car. As soon as I hung up with her, I called Medgar because I needed the results of that fucking DNA test on "Mrs. Black." When I gave it more thought, I remembered that Medgar has a rapid response test that takes about two hours for processing. It had actually been three hours, so he should have had something for me. I needed answers asap.

Chapter 6
Medgar

As I was printing the results of the DNA test that Vivian requested earlier, her name flashed across the screen of my ringing cell phone. I was actually glad that she was calling, because I was most certain that she told me that her client was a female. However, the results of the test revealed that *she* is a *he*. It looked like my friend may have a bigger mystery on her hands. She's going to trip even more when she learns that this fool is married. With all of Vivian's daddy issues, I just know that she's going to be livid. I hope this doesn't awaken Queen, because that bitch is something else...

"Medgar!" Vivian yelled before I could even place my phone up to my ear.

"Hey girl! I was actually about to call you... Is everything okay?" I asked because it seemed that she needed to tell me something that couldn't wait.

"Um... let's see... Fuck no everything is NOT okay! I'm sitting on a broken bench downtown with a swollen ankle and bruised ego! I just busted my ass running because I accidentally ran into that damn client that I called you about earlier. Have you gotten the results of the test?"

"Wow, I hope you're okay. Do I need to come get you?" I asked trying to prolong releasing the results.

"No, but thanks. Maria is actually on her way to get me. Have you processed that DNA yet? I think that Mrs. Black is actually a man. Unless she has an identical twin brother, I'm pretty sure I just saw her... his ass working at a construction site downtown."

"Well, since you're already sitting down. I guess I can confirm that you are right. I was just printing the results when you called. Mrs. Black is indeed a man – a married man at that. *His* real name is Tyrone Blackshire. He has been married to Tosha Gay Blackshire for fifteen years, and they have three teenage kids together. He owns a construction company, and he works back and forth between Shreveport and Chicago. His family actually lives in Chicago. He and his wife have had a shaky marriage because she always catches him cheating or being inappropriate with women. Tosha actually kicked one of his mistresses' ass and landed herself a battery case. Her reason for kicking the lady's ass was included in the report."

"Damn, that system sure does pull up every detail on folks. That's why I'm glad to have you on my team."

"Well, you know court records are public information. Do you have any idea why he came to visit you? Does his wife's name sound familiar? What are you gonna do about this person? Whatever you do, just please make sure Queen doesn't drive you to killing anybody this time."

"Believe it or not, I have no idea how I'm going to handle this. No, his wife's name does not sound familiar. Did the system display a picture of her, by chance?"

"Actually, it did. My fax machine is down right now, and I'm headed out of town for a few days. I'll leave a note for my secretary to fax it to you as soon as it's back up. You just make sure you control Queen," I said half-jokingly, but so serious.

The last time Viv got angry, Queen tortured a man so bad that he needed stitches in his backside. I can't say that he didn't deserve it though. He was a deacon at the church, and he was caught trying to rape an under aged girl. The child's mother took her to Vivian for counseling. Somehow Vivian got them to release a picture of him, and Queen handled the rest.

"Queen and I will be okay. Besides, we can't move prematurely. I need to figure out what's really going on right now. You enjoy your trip. I'll wait for your secretary to call me. Meanwhile, I need to book a flight to Chicago," Vivian said as we both said goodbye and hung up.

I guess I'll be hearing the explosion with that new information by the time I return from my business trip. Maybe I'll get my secretary to prolong sending the file over. Then again, Viv is going to do the fool now or later. Considering that my fax machine isn't really broken, I'll send it right over and put Viv on auto-block for a few days. I may as well get this shit out of the way now and hope that it has died down by the time I get back.

Chapter 7

Tosha

My husband is cheating on me. I've known for a long time, but I chose to ignore it. That's what my mom and aunts did. They ignored when their husbands were running the streets with other women, because all of their bills were paid. They also enjoyed nice houses, luxury vehicles, and expensive jewelry. I guess that was compensation for turning a blind eye to their cheating ways and a deaf ear to being called the wrong name during sex. I really don't understand how they easily accepted their husbands – the men who vowed to love and respect them – giving their love, time, and sex to some tramp in the streets.

Every time Tyrone boards the plane to Louisiana, I wonder if he has another family there or if he really is working his construction business. I've considered following him, but I'm not really sure if I'm ready to face the music. I thought about hiring a private detective to follow him around. I would have to use someone that lives in Shreveport because I can't afford to fly one there from Chicago and pay for their services. I may even start getting counseling. I'll use a fake name because I'm not sure who all he knows in Louisiana.

When I was at the nail salon, I overheard some women discussing a great counselor in Louisiana that either helps you repair your marriage, or she empowers you to handle your man properly. The way they stressed the word *handle* made me even more curious about her services - especially since Tyrone has been *handling* that hoe Debbie down the street for the past six months. I see the way they look at each other when we attend the monthly neighborhood association meetings. It's like they can't wait to tear each other apart again. On top of that, each household brings a covered dish, and she just happens to always bring one of Tyrone's favorite dishes.

This motherfucker doesn't even like to eat from other folks' houses, but he insists on tasting whatever she brings. I'm sure that's not all he's tasting. Her ass brought some rice pilaf to the first meeting she attended. I was late coming to the meeting, but when I walked up I saw his ass in her face saying how much he liked rice pilaf. He was sure to stress the word *like* so his tongue could lick his top lip. Everyone in the room saw it happening, and they elbowed each other and whispered.

At the time, that bitch didn't know he was married. Therefore, she didn't see the crowd part as I made my way towards them. She was enjoying the show, so she had the nerve to position her fork to feed my husband. Before she could meet his mouth, I took that whole plate and smashed it in his face. Then, I said, "That's how you feed the motherfucker!" As he stood there cleaning up the mixture of rice, snot, and blood from his face, she tried to jump up like she wanted to do something. I let that hoe know that he's my husband and her best option was to sit down and stay out of this shit. She politely took her seat and looked the other way.

Meanwhile, he stood there with an ass look on his face as he cleaned himself up. I politely grabbed my shit and left. You could have heard a rat piss on cotton as I walked out the door. That was one of the many times that he's embarrassed me by flirting with other women in my presence, but it damn sure wasn't the last. He assures me that he's not interested in them; he just likes to flirt. However, I can't talk to the mailman for more than thirty seconds before he brings his ass down the driveway to chime in on the conversation. I actually like that he gets jealous, but I wish he would stop the flirting and cheating. I really love my husband, and I want my marriage to work. He's the only man that I've ever been with sexually. I wouldn't even know what to do with myself if he left me.

My husband is truly irresistible. He's 6'3" tall with long dreadlocks and smooth chocolate skin. His body is athletic and his muscles are firm from the heavy lifting and construction work. I try to keep my 5'6" 160-pound frame looking right. My natural TWA fits my pretty caramel face perfectly. The sexual chemistry still flows between us, but he just can't seem to remember our commitment to each other. I've tried counseling with him. We've gone on vacation with other couples. I've even installed a spinning pole in our bedroom, and I'm not afraid to climb to the top and work my way back down. However, he's just not satisfied with having just me.

My girlfriends have offered suggestions on how I can please him. Candy suggested that I give him a threesome. She even offered to join us. She said that it would be best if I included one of my friends because I know they won't hurt me by sneaking around with him. I've been considering the idea. A threesome was something that my mom and aunts would never do, and their husbands continued to mess around on them. Maybe if I give Tyrone one, he'll see that I'll do anything for him. My best friend Amber thinks I'm crazy for thinking like that, but what does she know? She can barely keep a man herself. Candy is beautiful and outgoing, and all the men love her. I think she has the right idea about my marriage. I just might take her up on her offer.

Our anniversary is approaching, and I keep hinting around at wanting to take a trip to celebrate our sixteenth year of marriage. Tyrone claims he has to work and won't be able to take the trip. Part of me believes that he's trying to surprise me for a change. The other part of me hopes he won't disappoint me once again. Either way, I need to get to Louisiana to see that counselor. I try so hard to be a good wife, and he insists on living life just for himself. I feel so weak and hopeless, but it's what I'm supposed to do. He's given me the finer things like this house, any car I've ever wanted, jewelry, and so much more. The least I could do is allow him a little freedom. I know we've been married for over a decade now, but he will eventually get it out of his system. Meanwhile, I'll continue to be strong as I try to save my marriage and fight off his bitches. Maybe Vivian McQueen can help me figure it all out.

Chapter 8

Tyrone

I have an addiction to women. I have been married for sixteen years, but I can't seem to be faithful to my wife. She's a great mother, a great wife, a great cook, and a great lover. Yet, that's not enough for me. My cheating ways have gotten me into so much shit over the years, but there's just something about the feeling of new pussy that has a hold on me. I'm currently juggling three women, including my wife. It's easy for me to balance the three relationships because my two side pieces live in Shreveport where I work, and my wife never leaves Chicago for anything. I had a fourth one that lived down the street, but I had to leave her alone after my wife shoved food in my face because she caught her feeding me. Debbie is still very tempting, but I know Tosha would kill her if I got caught up with her again. I'm not worried about her hurting me or leaving me, because she loves me too much ever do anything like that.

My two side pieces are another story. They actually work together and have been friends for many years. I met Cheyenne on a dating site, and we are scheduled to see each other on Friday. I met Marissa on a renovation job, but I had no idea that they knew each other until after Cheyenne and I talked more online. By the time I realized that they knew each other, my feelings had already developed for Cheyenne. She talks about Marissa nonstop. She even suggested that we meet each other this weekend. Luckily, Marissa won't be in town. I'm hoping that I can get them both in the bed at the same time since they're so close. That'll eventually come. As long as I can keep up with both of their schedules, I should be able to pull this off. I just need to keep my wife under control, because she has been acting strange lately.

Tosha has been trying new things in the bedroom, and I even found a leather whip in her vanity drawer. Right next to it was a business card from a counselor in Shreveport. It didn't say what type of counselor the lady is, and I don't understand why she can't see a counselor in Chicago. I made a mental note of the name and began to do my own research. It turns out that the counselor is some psycho broad that teaches women how to be powerful through sex and some weird ass dominatrix type shit. That could explain why Tosha thought she was going to stick her fingers in my ass the other night. She had me tied to the bed, and I was enjoying her sucking my dick from the back until I felt the lube running down the crack of my ass. I let it slide at first, but then she started massaging too close to my asshole. Before I knew it, I accidentally mule kicked her off the bed. I quickly apologized, but she had already gotten embarrassed and ran out the room.

I haven't told her that I paid a visit to the counselor, Vivian. I had to disguise myself as a woman because she doesn't counsel with men at all. A few men in the city have heard all sorts of wild stories about things she's done to men. The thing is, no one knows for a fact how true the stories are. They even mentioned some kind of Queen package that costs thousands of dollars, but it's worth every penny. Her secretary is trained on how to screen potential clients. She won't release any information whatsoever. I stopped by there one day dressed as my normal self, and Maria – the assistant – wouldn't budge. She kept saying that it was a women's counseling facility and she could not help me.

I was able to steal a brochure when she went to get something off the printer for someone who called the phone. From the brochure, I learned of the services that are offered. I also realized that I needed a woman to help me get inside to see Vivian. I needed to figure out just who had my wife violating me like that. I thought about asking one of my side pieces to check it out for me, but then they would know I'm married. I didn't want to ruin my fun so quickly. That's when I decided to disguise myself as a woman named Mrs. Black. I pretended like I heard of the services from a close friend that used the company before.

When Maria tried to reject me because I didn't have an appointment, I slid her two crisp one-hundred dollar bills to let me in to speak with Vivian. I assured her that I wouldn't be long. I even nibbled on her ear lobe as I whispered my request to her. I took a chance of being slapped, but I needed to try whatever I could to get inside Vivian's office. My plan worked, and I was able to see the face behind my wife's new actions.

I entered the office like a boss, although I was captivated by Vivian's beauty. I made a mental note to ask her on a date after I figured out her plans for my wife. I didn't ask many questions, nor did I say much to her. I just played the role of this mysterious woman and felt her out a bit. Her presence was strong, but I could tell that I was getting to her. She's used to being in control, yet I took over her office. She gave me an application for her services. It was ten pages long and required a commitment to secrecy before starting services with her. That's probably why I wasn't able to find out anything concrete about her services.

When I left her office, I disposed of my women's attire in the bathroom trash can. I did that just in case Vivian or anyone else had their eyes on the Mrs. Black that had just left her office. I quickly hopped in my matte black work truck and headed to my construction site just a few blocks over. I planned to keep an eye on Ms. Vivian for a while. I also need to find someone to watch Tosha while I'm away from Chicago. I don't need her slipping out of the city or getting any more ideas. That taming shit is for the birds and those white folks. Black people don't get all into that weird ass dominatrix shit. This ain't no Fifty Colors of Tosha or whatever she's thinking.

Chapter 9

The Chamber

Because it's hot outside, most of the men were on their worst behaviors. It's something about seeing women in short shorts and swimsuits that makes men forget that they are actually married with kids. Between suntan lotion and condensation on beer bottles, men often slip off their wedding rings and lose a bit of their minds. This was the case with the police officer, Malcolm, that was being punished by his wife. After being called to a domestic dispute at a public swimming pool, Malcolm managed to exchange numbers with the female involved in the dispute while her husband was handcuffed in the back of the police cruiser.

According to the lie that he told his wife when she found the number inside his cop car, Malcolm needed her number just in case he needed her to make a statement. Apparently her statement at the pool wasn't enough. However, he didn't seem to need her husband's phone number for any statements about the heated argument at the pool. Those phone calls and text messages regarding her statement led to lunch dates, secret meetings, and eventually hotel visits.

Like any other dumb ass cheating man, he stayed out late, suddenly started going to the gym and never lost weight, and he kept his phone on silent and tucked deep in pockets. His wife noticed the changes in his behavior right away, but she continued to be a great wife as usual. The house was always clean, the kids were near perfect, his food was always hot, and the sex was on demand. Malcolm couldn't have asked for a better wife and life. Yet he still wanted to test the waters. He knew Shuntel was crazy, but he didn't think she'd follow through on her threats of making him pay for the pain he was causing her.

As Malcolm laid on his back, strapped to a cold metal table, he regretted ever taking the call at the pool that day. His wife was dressed in a red leather catsuit wearing six-inch stiletto boots and holding a spiked whip. Her breasts were fully exposed through two holes in the catsuit. The music was loud as various cheating songs blared through speakers. Each time the song changed, his wife's rage increased. While Atlantic Starr sung *Secret Lovers*, Shuntel attached clamps to his nipples as she gently kissed him from his neck down to the tip of his dick.

While she teased him by licking up and down his shaft to his balls and his asshole, she flipped the switch on the machine that was connected to the clamps. Within seconds a wave of shock shot through Malcolm's body, and he let out a loud, bitchy scream. You would have thought a woman saw a damn mouse the way he yelped like a fucking girl. Seeing his squirming and shaking like he was having a seizure sent Shuntel into a hysterical laughing fit. Onlookers thought she was crazy, but she didn't care. She continued to laugh as she flipped the switch off and on, sending fresh waves of electrical currents through his body.

"That's how your motherfucking ass made me feel each time you climbed in our bed and held me tightly! I had currents of love flowing through my heart as you kissed me and told me how blessed you were to have me as a wife! I knew you were cheating, but I hoped that our love for each other would have made you rethink your foolish decision to fuck up our marriage and our home. You were my first everything. I trusted you with my life, and you made a fucking fool of me with that ugly ass young slut fucking bitch!"

As Shuntel continued to rant about how badly he hurt her, she failed to realize that his moans were starting to fade.

"You saw everything that my father did to my mother while we were in high school, and you still did the shit to me! You saw how your daddy cheated on your mom and made babies in the streets, and you still cheated on me!"

Each time she added an offense to Malcolm's list, she amped up the currents a little more.

"Say something motherfucker! Anything! Why did you do this to US!? You were my EVERYTHING! I helped you stash fucking drugs and money from a drug bust. I jeopardized my life and freedom for you! I put our kids in danger of losing both of us, and you just had to throw it all away for a married ugly ass side piece! Answer me!"

Malcolm's body laid limp on the table. He was no longer conscious, and he was barely breathing. Shuntel finally realized something was wrong and quickly turned off the machine.

"Noooo!! Baby! Wake up, honey! I'm so sorry! Wake up!! Malcolm! Baby, don't leave me!"

While Malcolm fought for his life, his wife quickly disconnected the nipple clamps and unstrapped him from the table. She didn't know what to do. Queen would kill her if she called for an ambulance and exposed the activities of the queendom. She began performing CPR as some of the onlookers stood by whispering. Others ran for help while a few got dressed and made quick exits in case the cops came. As Shuntel continued chest compressions, her mind began to flashback to the scenes of Malcolm wining and dining his mistress. She thought about the countless times that she watched him make passionate love to the woman who had stolen her husband and ruined her life. The sounds of Malcolm moaning and calling her by his mistress's name replayed in her ear repeatedly.

As Kelly Price sung *As We Lay* through the speakers of the chamber, Shuntel slowly stopped giving him CPR. She debated if she should save him or let him die on the table. As she contemplated her next move, she walked over to the window and drew the curtains so that the people watching her would not be able to see inside the chamber any longer. Then, she returned to the table and slapped the shit out of Malcolm. He let out a low moan, but he didn't wake up. At least she knew he wasn't dead, so she opened a bottle of ice cold water and poured it all over his face. Since he liked bitches at swimming pools, his ass was going to drown.

The cold water did the trick, and Malcolm woke up coughing and choking on the water that had gotten into his nose and mouth.

"Fucking crazy bitch," he mumbled as he rolled over and continued to cough. "Why are you doing this to me? This freaky shit is getting out of hand. What the fuck is wrong with you? I thought we were supposed to be enjoying some freaky shit and swinging at this resort. If I didn't know any better, I'd think yo' ass is trying to kill me!"

Again, Shuntel laughed hysterically. This time, tears streamed down her cheeks as she grabbed the remote control from a drawer and turned on the projector.

"We're going to do some freaky shit alright... What's wrong with me? Ha, you know exactly what the fuck is wrong with me! Your cheating, gonorrhea, chlamydia, and lies are what's wrong with me!" she yelled as she played the slide show of pictures she got from Medgar's private investigation work.

Shuntel continued to cry as Malcolm sat naked on the table trying to think of an explanation for the images that played while Billy Paul's voice sung *Me and Mrs. Jones.* There were images of Malcolm and his bitch sharing a corndog at the park. They were dressed alike and hugged up as if they were truly a couple. The next slide showed them entering the Vintage Steakhouse on Valentine's Day. Shuntel remembered that night vividly. Malcolm was supposed to be out of town at a work training, so he promised to make the night up to her when he returned. She allowed him to put on the charade of being so sad to leave, but Medgar had already told her that he spotted Malcolm and his mistress together making reservations earlier that day. Tears continued to stream down her cheeks, and her breathing rapidly increased. She felt herself getting angry, but she tried her best to keep calm.

She had watched the footage a dozen times before, but there was something about seeing that dumb ass look on Malcolm's face that made her want to unload the nine millimeter gun in her boots on his ass. He sat there looking ugly as hell trying to squeeze out some tears. Shuntel just stared at him in disgust as she walked around him slowly. He didn't move a muscle because he was afraid of whoever this person was that had taken over his wife. When Shuntel got in front of Malcolm, she bent down as if she was about to suck his exposed dick. She rubbed his thighs with one hand and grabbed his dick with the other hand. As his dick grew into an erection, she sung to it like she was singing on a microphone.

"Me and Mrs. Mrs. Hoe from the Pooooll... We got a thinnnggg going on."

As Shuntel sung into her husband's dick mic, she purposely let her tongue graze his tip. Each time her tongue touched him, Malcolm's dick would jump with pleasure. The slick swipes became sensual sucks and slurps. Malcolm wasn't sure what was going on, but he couldn't help but enjoy his wife's warm mouth on him.

Shuntel sucked and sucked while Malcolm moaned and moaned. As soon as Billy Paul sung the last word to that horrible cheating ass song, Shuntel gripped Malcolm's nuts as tightly as she could and bit his dick until she drew blood! Malcolm let out a high pitched scream, and Shuntel grabbed her shit and exited the chamber before he was able to knock her ass out for biting him. An image of Shuntel in bed with Malcolm's best friend was the last picture in the slide show. *Revenge is the sweetest joy next to getting dick,* she thought to herself as she fled to safety.

Chapter 10

Cheyenne

After a long week, it's finally time for me to meet my computer love. We decided to meet for dinner and drinks. If the evening goes well, we'll go check out M.A.D. 1st Friday at Jazzy's Lounge. I've been a couple of time with my clients, and it's so relaxing and fun. Miguel is into the arts just as I am, so I'm sure he would enjoy himself. I decided to drive myself to the date rather than using the limo service. Still, my cousin plans to send a couple of her guys to randomly check on me. I've given her all of the details for the night, and I packed my pepper spray just in case Miguel turns out to be a madman. We agreed to meet at the restaurant at seven o'clock. I wanted to get there early so I could see if I needed to flee the parking lot and never look back or remove my thong and hope to get laid.

I wore my sexy black dashiki dress and braided my hair into an elegant goddess braid. I wanted to show off my nice body and long legs while still representing my culture. Miguel said that he would be driving a matte black Infiniti QX80. I told him that I would be in my red

Mercedes, but I drove Marissa's purple Maserati instead.

As I sat in the parking lot waiting for my date, I watched couples come and go. Some of the couples looked great together with their coordinated colors. Others looked like they were forced to be with each other because of the kids. I saw gay couples that seemed to be much happier than the heterosexual couples. I even saw an older lady cursing her husband out because he was walking too slow. The poor man was even on a walker, but that didn't stop his wife from giving him the blues. I guess that was payback from all the hell he could have put her through in their marriage. The funny thing is that he talked trash right back as he continued to move at a snail's pace toward the restaurant.

After enjoying the couples' sitcoms for almost half an hour, my entertainment was interrupted by Miguel's vehicle pulling into the parking lot. His windows were tinted so dark that it had to be illegal, so I could not get a sneak preview of the goods. I watched him back in and park about four spaces down from me. He opened the mirror in his sun visor, and the vanity lights allowed me to get a glimpse of him. From what I could see, he had long dreads and appeared to have nice shoulders. *This dress might come in handy after all,* I thought to myself. I continued to watch him as he checked his nose for little friends and checked his teeth.

For a second, I thought I saw a ring sparkle on his left ring finger, but I couldn't be too sure due to the tint. *Surely this man isn't married. Maybe I'm just being paranoid. They are not all the same. He is not one of the guys from your past. You two have gotten along so well in the chats. He would have told you if he was married.* I tried to reassure myself that my computer love is a perfect as I have imagined him to be.

He finally stepped out of his vehicle and I instantly forgot all of my crazy thoughts. This man was fine! He was dressed in a crisp black button down shirt with slim-fitted slacks and a nice pair of loafers. His shirt hugged his biceps and shoulders perfectly, and his ass complimented his slacks just right. His long dreads were pulled back in a wavy ponytail that extended down the middle of his back. If he smells as good as he looks, he's in for a long night.

I waited until he was inside the restaurant before I got out of the car. I needed to make sure all my shit was straight before we finally met face to face. I sprayed a couple of extra squirts of perfume between my perky breasts and between my thighs. I made sure my titties were sitting pretty and my butt had just enough jiggle to grab his attention. I strutted in my six-inch stilettos as if I was walking down the runway to become the next top model. I had to practice my stride in the parking lot so that I could be in full force by the time Miguel saw me. By the time I reached the door of the restaurant, he surprisingly greeted me. I was a little embarrassed because I didn't know how long he had been watching me.

"Hello, Cheyenne. How are you?" Miguel asked in the sexiest, deepest voice I had ever heard.

"Hi... You must be Miguel? How did you know it was me?"

"Well, my beautiful queen... How many sisters wear dashiki dresses and goddess braids for a night on the town?" he asked as he grabbed my hand and kissed it gently.

"Ha... I guess you're right. Thanks for the compliment. You look great yourself."

You look good enough to eat! Let's skip dinner and get straight to the damn dessert! I thought as I tried my best not to get high off the scent of Polo Red coupled with his sexy looks. *Damn bih... You hit this jackpot with this one.*

"I've already requested a table. I didn't see your car outside, so I wanted to be sure that you didn't have to wait when you arrived. Are you okay?"

"Yes. I'm fine. Why do you ask?"

"You seem a little preoccupied. Do I look that terrible?" Miguel joked to lighten up the tension.

I guess my thoughts were written all over my face.

"Oh no. You're fine. I mean... I'm fine... Uh I just had a long day, but I'm much better now. How long is the wait?" I asked trying to change the subject.

Before he could answer, the hostess came back to seat us. She escorted us to a private table towards the back of the restaurant. As we were walking, I could feel Miguel's eyes all over me. I made every step count as I took long sensual strides. When we sat down, I noticed that he kept his hands underneath the table. *I bet this fool really is married. Damn you, Cheyenne! You sure know how to pick them. Maybe they're separated or on bad terms. What am I saying? Separated is still married damn it. My parents were still married when my daddy decided to fuck his secretary. Don't go down that same path,* I thought as I tried to find something wrong with him.

"Amber will be your server. Can I start you off with something to drink? We have happy hour going until 8:30. It includes wine, draft beers, and well drinks" the hostess said.

"You first," Miguel offered.

"I'll have a glass of White Zinfandel, please."

"I'll have the same."

"Alright. I'll get it right over to you."

We sat in silence for the first few seconds before I broke the ice.

"How was your trip?"

"It was smooth. No complaints. I was just anxious to see you. It could have crash landed here, and that would have been fine with me," he flirted.

"Oh really," I blushed. "I'm glad to finally see the man behind the screen. You look different from what I imagined."

"What did you imagine?"

"You want the truth?"

"Please."

"I just knew you would be some fat nerdy guy with a big belly, scruffy beard, and cow licks."

We both laughed and awkwardly grabbed hands, and then quickly pulled away.

"Nah. You got the wrong guy, love. You actually look exactly how I imagined. You have your Lauryn Hill and Erykah Badu thing going, and I love it. You are a beautiful queen, and I'm glad I fell in your DM."

"I'm glad, too."

We continued the usual conversation for a first date. We talked about our childhoods, siblings, college days, work, and even the upcoming election. He finally showed his left hand, and there was no ring. I thought I saw a faint tan line, but I couldn't really tell and didn't want to stare. I decided to drop that idea for a second, and I just enjoyed a wonderful evening with a gorgeous man. I couldn't wait to tell Marissa that I may have finally found a love of my own.

Chapter 11
Marissa

Despite having to endure my hating cousins from L.A., I actually enjoyed my family this weekend. I didn't get a chance to talk to Tyrone much because he was occupied with the big project at work. He would miss my calls and then text me back within ten minutes. That was strange, but I allowed it considering how busy he has been with work. Sometimes I swear he's married, but he assures me that he isn't. When I ask why he hasn't invited me to his home yet, he claims that he's remodeling and his house is a mess. He swears that he'll invite me over as soon as he gets everything in order. I'm not going to push the issue because I don't want him to think that I don't trust him.

Cheyenne finally met her online boo in person this weekend. She has not shut up about how sexy and charming he is. They went to dinner and hung out all night before he drove back home. She has been going on and on about how great he smells and his soft lips. Coincidentally, her guy is also dark with dreads like Tyrone. His name is Miguel and he's Dominican and Black. Although I'm happy for her, I hope that Miguel isn't cuter than Tyrone. I would never hear the end of that. She wants our beaus to meet so we can double date and enjoy us both finally having pure love in our lives. I'm looking forward to meeting the guy that has my friend walking around with little hearts floating around her head.

She'll actually get to meet Tyrone sooner than expected. He's stopping by the shop next week so we can decide which area he and his crew will be renovating first. Cheyenne and I are usually slower on Wednesdays and Thursdays. Those are the days we see appointment clients only. Walk-ins are welcome any other day of the week. I told Tyrone to stop by on one of those days, and we can do a walk-through between clients. This would also give me a chance to introduce him to Cheyenne. I'm slightly nervous about the introduction, because I don't want her to find anything wrong with him. We like to assess each other's men to ensure that we aren't being played. I haven't told her that I have a suspicion of him being married because I really like him. Plus, I don't want to hear her mouth about what our mothers endured and how we shouldn't do the same thing to other women. I value her opinion, but sometimes I don't always want to know the truth. Maybe she won't be so opinionated since she has a new man and all.

***

As I pulled up to Xpressions after a quick break to grab some lunch, a black convertible Jaguar parked next to me. The lady driving the car got out and went to the door of the salon. She let out a sigh of disappointment when she realized the door was locked. Before she could walk off, I quickly got out of my car.

"Hi. May I help you?"

"Oh. Hi. Yes, I was wondering if they take walk-ins. I'm not from the area, and I need a refill on my gel manicure. I checked local reviews, and they all pointed me to this place. Do you work here?" the lady asked.

"Yes, I do. I'm actually one of the owners. Thanks for taking the advice of the reviews. My name is Marissa. We do take walk-ins. I was kind of slow today, so I ran to get some lunch. We're usually open through lunch. Please forgive me. My partner should be in shortly as well."

"Girl, it's no problem. You have to eat. My name is Tosha. I can wait until you're done eating. I'm not in a hurry. I'm actually surprising my husband. His construction company has a contract here. We're from Chicago. This is like his second home."

I immediately started choking on my tea when I heard that.

"Oh my! Are you okay?" Tosha asked.

"Yes... I'm fine," I said between coughs. "My tea must have gone down the wrong pipe as the old folks say."

"You scared me for a moment. I thought I was going to have to call for back up," she joked.

"Haha. No, I'm okay. What did you say your husband does, again?"

"He owns a construction company."

"Oh okay. That's awesome. And, you said you're surprising him? I'm sure he's going to be excited to see you."

I tried my best to keep my composure, but I was fuming on the inside. *Is this Tyrone's wife? Is he really married? What are the odds of my boyfriend's wife coming to my shop from Chicago? Does she know about us? Hell, I didn't know anything about a wife until now. I mean, I had my suspicions. Did her intuition lead her to me? Ugh! I need to call his ass right now! I should just tell her everything! Yes, that's what I'll do! Wait... what if she's armed and she knows about us? Hell, I'm innocent. She can't harm me. On second thought, let's just see if she knows anything.* My thoughts were running rampant as I tried to figure out how to approach this situation.

"Um, let me get you soaking while I knock out this sandwich. While I'm getting you set up, pick your color. Our gel section is just over there."

"Wow, you have a huge selection. I'm impressed. I love to see black businesses with their shit in order."

Is this bitch trying to be funny? Let me calm down. I could just be jumping to conclusions based on my suspicions.

"Yea girl. We have to beat the competition and work twice as hard as the white folks. There's no such thing as black privilege."

"I know that's right, chile."

While Tosha browsed our gel nail polish selection, I prepared my station to let her soak her nails. I glanced at her occasionally, and I couldn't help but notice her simple beauty. She had a beautiful complexion and a nice athletic body. She didn't wear makeup, but her flawless skin didn't need it anyway. If my Tyrone was really her husband, I wonder why he would cheat on a woman so beautiful. These damn men just have to have to be greedy.

My appetite disappeared as my heart settled in my stomach from the pain of my boyfriend possibly being married. I decided to pick Tosha for information while her nails soaked.

"I guess I had too much tea and spoiled my appetite. I'll just keep you company while your polish softens. So, how long do you plan to stay in Shreveport?"

"I'll only be here for a couple of days. My husband and his crew have a couple of apartments here until their big job is done downtown. I've checked into the Hilton near his construction site. My flight came in this morning. I tried calling him earlier, but he didn't answer. I figured he was busy, so I decided to do a little shopping and pamper myself after that long flight and a couple of delays."

I cringed each time she mentioned more details that confirmed my Tyrone as her husband. Still, I played it off and continued my line of questioning as I worked on her nails.

"Do you want French tips, or the full nail painted white?"

"I'll take just the tips and a design. You can do whatever you want on the design," Tosha said with a smile.

"Awesome," I replied and forced a smile.

I decided not to ask any more questions about her husband because I didn't want to cause her to become suspicious. I continued her nails, and we talked about general girl stuff, the presidential race between a bad candidate and a terrible racist, sexist, incestuous candidate, and life as a minority business owner. Tosha seemed like a nice woman. However, I couldn't wait to talk to Tyrone's lying ass. I wasn't even prepared to tell Cheyenne that my relationship failed before she even got the chance to meet him. I didn't want to scare her away from her new love. Sadly, I knew this shit was too good to be true.

Chapter 12
Tosha

Since Tyrone was inconsistent with answering my phone calls, I decided to surprise him in Shreveport. I also wanted to use this time to reach out the counselor that everyone thought was so great. Since it was after noon when I arrived and got settled into my hotel, I decided to do a little shopping and get my nails done. I wanted to look sexy for my husband when he saw me after work. I went to a nail salon about ten miles from his construction site. The owner was really nice, but she seemed as if she knew Tyrone. There was just something about the way she choked on her tea when I mentioned what kind of work my husband does. She asked me a few questions, but I could tell that she wanted to know more. I played it cool and waited for her to drop some kind of clue that she does know him. I wasn't able to gather much information, but I don't think that really means much. I know how much Southern women love men from out of town. I'm sure she's crossed paths with him at some point in this small ass town. No worries... I'll be sure to pay her another visit before I head back home.

After a couple of failed attempts to reach Tyrone on his cell, I gave him one more call before I was going to head to his site. Luckily, he answered this time.

"Hello? Baby, can you hear me?" Tyrone said over the loud sound of hammering in the background.

"Hey! Yes, I can hear you. I've been calling you all day. I was beginning to worry. Have you been super busy today?"

"Yea, it's been crazy, and my phone was charging in my truck. Is everything okay?"

"Everything is fine. I was just missing you and wondering what you're doing for dinner."

"Dinner? I wish I was eating you, but me and the guys might watch a game at a sports bar."

"Eating me, huh? That sounds like a date," I flirted back with my husband.

"I guess you plan to SnapChat me that pussy?" he joked.

"I'll do you even better and let you eat me tonight at the Hilton downtown."

"Hilton? Downtown where?"

"Shreveport. Surprise!"

Tyrone was so silent on the other end of the phone that I had to look at my phone to see if the call had dropped.

"Hello? Babe, are you there?"

"Uh yea, I'm here. My bad. You're in Shreveport?" he asked in a flat tone.

"Yes... Is that a problem?" I asked disappointedly.

"No, baby! Of course not! That's great! I can't wait to see you. Why didn't you tell me you were coming in town? I would have cleared my schedule for you."

"I wanted to surprise you. I know it can be hard on you traveling back and forth constantly. I needed a break from work, so I decided to come to you instead. Besides, I know you need to finish up on this job, and traveling tends to slow you down."

"That's sweet of you. When did you arrive?"

"I got in this morning, but I wanted to get cute for you. So I went shopping and got my nails done at a nice place in town. I think it's called Xpressions or something like that. The owner, Marissa, was really cool and did a great job on my nails."

"Xpressions? Wow," Tyrone said in a surprised tone.

"What's the 'wow' for? Is that place good?"

"Oh... no. I mean, yea. It's good. It's fine. Um... Nah, I actually have to go check it out because they need some work done. It's just weird that you ended up there on your first try. There are lots of nail salons all over town. That's all."

"Hmm. That's weird. I mentioned what you do and she never said anything about getting any work done," I said as I grew suspicious.

"Don't start, Tosha," Tyrone griped.

"Don't start what? Damn, I can't ask you any questions? Wow. Sorry," I snapped.

"Baby, ask me anything you want. I just know how you can get sometimes. Look, I'm glad you made it in safely. Thanks for surprising me. I'll try to wrap things up within the next hour or two, and I'll link up with you."

"Okay. You are staying with me tonight, right?"

"Of course I am. You think I'm gonna let my sexy ass wife stay in a hotel alone? You gotta be crazy. I'll be there to eat that later, so be sure she's all shaved and cute for daddy," he flirted.

"Mmmm. I can't wait. I'll talk to you soon. I love you," I blushed as we hung up.

Tyrone had a way of turning me on and stopping me from chewing him out. Maybe I was overreacting based on his past, but something wasn't sitting well with me about his job with Xpressions. It looks like I need to chip my nail polish and have it repaired before I leave town. Meanwhile, I need to shave Ms. Jaguar and get ready for my husband to blow my back out tonight. It's been a long time, and I need a touch up. I'll deal with my suspicions later, and I'll be sure to contact that counselor tomorrow.

Chapter 13
Vivian

It's been a busy week dealing with Queen and the Queendom. We just accepted a few new ladies as madams, and they are hungry for healing. We've had to fast-track them on the orientation process so they could get started before they end up hurting their men. One of our most recent women bit a main vein in her husband's penis, and he wanted to press charges. Our physician was able to do an emergency surgery on him, but we are out of a lot of money to keep him quiet. Queen managed to convince him that he deserved to feel his wife's rage because of the pain he caused her with his cheating ways. At first he wasn't buying it, but Queen counted out fifteen thousand dollars in hush money and changed his tune. The victim and his wife have agreed to go their separate ways, and Malcolm, the husband, knows not to breathe a word of the ordeal to anyone. Their marriage will end based on irreconcilable differences, and Shuntel, the wife, will become a part-time madam at the Queendom.

After spending so much time dealing with that chaotic situation, I am relieved to be back in my office amid a pile of paperwork. I read through the fax that Medgar sent to me, and I am blown away its contents. Don't get me wrong. I've dealt with married couples that are experiencing infidelity. However, I've never had the male to dress up as a female to pay me a visit. I can't help but wonder why he would go through such great lengths to disguise himself. I wonder if he knows that I'm the same woman that he flirted with a few months back. How long has he been planning to meet me? Better yet, what is his actual plan?

The ringing phone interrupted my thoughts. Maria picked up after two rings and buzzed my office seconds later.

"Excuse me, Viv. There's a Tosha Blackshire on Line 1. She's requesting an appointment for today or tomorrow. She says she'll only be in town for a few days. Your last client comes in at three o'clock today. That will leave you with two free hours. Do you want me to slide her in?" Maria asked.

"Did you say 'Tosha Blackshire' wants an appointment?" I asked to ensure that I was hearing Maria correctly.

"Yes ma'am. It looks like she's calling from a Chicago number. Do you want me to take a message?"

"Uh yea... Wait! No! No. That's fine. Let her come in this afternoon," I stammered.

"Are you sure?" Maria responded.

"No, I'm not, but I'm eager to know what's going on. So yes, let her come in today. Thanks, Maria," I said and clicked the line before she could say anything else.

***

My appointment with Tosha Blackshire finally rolled around. I decided to hold our meeting in the conference room to avoid being held captive just as I was when her husband came in disguise. When she entered the room, I noticed a unique beauty about her. She had a beautiful complexion and a nice, athletic body. Everything was in place from her natural hair to her nicely manicured nails. Based on her appearance, I couldn't see a reason for her husband to cheat on her. I decided to gather more of an opinion after speaking with her for a bit.

"Good afternoon, Mrs. Blackshire. What brings you here today? I don't usually accept last minute appointments, but Maria said that it seemed urgent. How may I help you?"

"Hi, Vivian. You can call me Tosha. I'm only in town for a couple of days, and I wanted to be sure to see you while I'm here. I'm from Chicago, but I've heard so much about you and your services."

"That's great. Chicago huh? Did you come to town just to see me? If so, do they not have counselors in Chicago?"

"Well, yes and no. Yes, I came in town to see you. I also came to see my husband. His construction company has a contract here. Yes, we do have counselors in Chicago. However, those counselors don't offer your services. My husband and I have been having issues for some time now. The issues have mainly been one-sided, and well... I'm tired of it. I'm sick of being his perfect little wife and secretary while he runs the streets fucking any woman who will give it up. I've fought for my marriage for years, and he's continued to lie and cheat on me. I need you to help me fix my marriage. I want control of my marriage."

"I see. How did you hear about my services?"

"I heard about you when I was at the nail salon back home. Someone gave me your card. I caught my husband looking at it, and he seemed nervous when I asked what he was doing and if he knew you. I initially assumed that you were another one of his women. Then, I thought he had plans to contact you to help us with our marriage. However, I learned through research that you don't counsel men. That made me revisit the thought of you being a side woman, so I decided to surprise my husband with this trip to your city. Once I got here, I asked around about you, and I learned that you play no games with men. I'm still confused on why my husband acted strangely when he saw your card, but I'm more interested in your services and my healing. Can you help me?"

80

"I see."

"You see? What do you see? Is that all you say? Never mind! I made a mistake coming here. This is a waste of time!"

Tosha began to quickly gather her things to leave, but my words interrupted her and she sat back down.

"Are you sure you want to do this?" I asked very calmly.

"I don't know what I'm sure of, but I know that I'm sick of his shit. Do you see these beautiful nails? His new bitch's business partner did them. She almost choked on her tea when I mentioned little details about my husband. I found information about their shop in the emails that she and my husband shared. He created a fake account and a new name. My husband has been communicating with his new fling for some time, and they finally met up a couple of days ago. Part of me wanted to pop up and ruin their date, but the other part didn't really want to see it. Therefore, I just let it happen... again... I let my husband woo another woman, while I sat back and did nothing."

I continued to listen as Tosha pitied herself for her horrible husband. While she spoke, I resisted the urge to vomit at the sad sight. There she was, a beautiful queen who allowed her no good ass husband to make her feel like a peasant. She continued on and on and on about her whore of a husband, and I imagined her in a sexy dominatrix outfit gaining power over her marriage. I envisioned her violating her husband with a piping hot glass dildo and a spiked paddle. I could see her being a woman of power with a bit a training. Although she ranted and raved about her marriage, she never shed one tear. That is what sealed the deal. That's what made me accept her as a client.

"And, even had the nerve to..."

"Enough!" I interrupted her whining. "I can't take another second of hearing you whine and complain. When are you leaving?"

"Excuse me? If you want me out of your office, just say it," she stammered.

"No. I'm asking when you're leaving Shreveport. I want to take you on a field trip. But, before we do, I'll need you to sign a non-disclosure agreement. That's IF you really want to find healing."

"I do. I do want healing, Vivian. I'm ready to heal. I'll be here until Thursday. I have plans with my husband tonight, but I'm free tomorrow."

"Cancel your plans with him. Tell him that you aren't feeling well."

"But, he's supposed to stay with me tonight at the hotel."

"Tell him that you went to ER, and you're contagious so he can't stay with you tonight. Tell him it's a 24-hour bug and you'll be better tomorrow," I said.

"Wow, you're quick on your feet. What if he tries to call me?"

"If you plan to roll with me, I need you to start thinking like a queen. Tell me what you will tell him," I said as I walked closely upon her.

I wanted her to feel uncomfortable to ensure that she could think under pressure. I got close enough for my breath to touch the back of her neck as I spoke.

"Tell me... what... you... will tell him," I whispered seductively.

"Um... Ahem... Um..." she stammered. "Um... I'll um. I'll be asleep. I'll tell him that the meds knocked me out," she finally said.

"Great! I'm ready when you're ready," I said as I stood upright and walked to the door.

Tosha squirmed in her seat for a moment, and then she gave me an embarrassed look as she grabbed her belongings and followed me out of the room. *She's going to be a lot of fun,* I thought with a slight chuckle.

Chapter 14
Marissa

After months of waiting for Tyrone to stay the night with me, the night has finally come. He said that one of his roommates is sick with a 24-hour bug, so he needed to crash at my place. I quickly agreed and even offered to cook dinner for him. Since we're usually slow at the beginning of the week, I left the salon early and decided to check out the new organic grocery store that was recently built. I picked up some fresh asparagus, sushi, and organic potatoes. Then, I went over to the fresh meat market and had a couple of thick steaks freshly sliced for us. I wanted to make this special night.

When I got home, I put the potatoes in the slow cooker and marinated the steaks for a couple of hours. Meanwhile, I made sure the house was spotless and smelling nice. I even installed my pole in my bedroom and practiced a few dance moves for later. I had been working on my upper body strength at the gym, so I climbing the pole wouldn't be an issue. My doorbell rung just as I was removing the steaks from the fridge to allow them to get to room temperature. I wasn't expecting Tyrone for another hour, so I didn't know who it could be.

"Just a minute!" I yelled as I walked to the living room and peeked out of the curtains.

Cheyenne's car was parked in the driveway, so I immediately opened the door.

"Hey girl, what's going on?" I asked as she barged her way past me.

"Hey chick. I was just out enjoying the nice evening and decided to stop by. Damn, girl. Something smells good. What do you have going?"

"Tyrone is coming by for dinner, and well... He's sleeping over."

"What!? Wow. I see things are getting serious between y'all. So, when do I get to meet my friend-in-law? It's only been what six months and shit," Cheyenne joked.

"Haha. It has not been six months. It's only been three, and we all keep missing each other. He's actually supposed to be here in an hour, but I'm gonna need you to be walking out the door as he's walking in. Unless..."

"Unless what? Nah, girl, I left that lifestyle back in my college days."

"Lifestyle? Girl, what the hell? Hell no! Not a threesome, bitch. I was thinking that you could invite Miguel over. Speaking of which... How did your date go?"

"Oh, my bad," she laughed. "It was perfect. He's hella cool, and gorgeous as fuck. He actually only came in town for a day just to see me, and then he drove back home. I'll see when he'll be back this way."

"Oh bummer. Okay, well just let me know so we can plan ahead."

"What are you cooking? Something smells delicious. You have the house all clean and shit. You must plan to fuck that man all over the place."

I laughed and high-fived her.

"Who says I haven't already fucked him everywhere, including that spot where you're sitting."

Cheyenne quickly jumped up and playfully hit me with the pillow that she was snuggling.

"You ole nasty heffa."

"Shut up. It's my house. I can do what I want where I want," I said and playfully stuck my tongue out at her. "Since you're here, you need to help me with this meal. And, I need you to tell me how my lil routine looks."

"Routine? Damn bihh... You're going all out. You must be expecting a ring or something."

"A ring? Hell no. I just like him. That's all."

"Girl, that's good. I haven't seen you like this in a long time. Cool. I can help you with whatever you need. Time is winding down, so let's get to it."

"Thanks, girl. That's why I fuck with you. You always have my back," I said as we turned on the music and began cooking a gourmet meal for my Tyrone.

"So, how has everything been going between you two? You're cooking and going all out. That must mean everything is on the up and up," Cheyenne said as she loaded the dishwasher.

"Girl, everything has been fine. At first, I had some suspicions about him, but I realized that I could be buggin' based on past relationships. Just when I thought I should explore other options, he called and told me that he wanted to spend the night with me. This will be the first time that he actually stays all night with me. Usually, he has to leave early because of work. He said something about his roommate being sick, so he needed to crash with me. I quickly accepted his offer, and here we are."

"Suspicions? What kind of suspicions did you have? I thought he was cool," she pried.

"Well, he is cool. I just had a problem with him not staying all night with me. I wanted to believe he is married, but we spend so much time together. Plus, I can call him at any hour of the night. Like I said, I could have just been trippin. You know I have issues with men. Anyway, these steaks are going to be on point, honey," I said in an attempt to change the subject.

After the strange client that I encountered at the shop today, I wanted to run the scenario by Cheyenne. I didn't plan to tell her that I thought it was Tyrone's wife, but I did want to get her thoughts on the situation. However, she was excited about Miguel, and I didn't want to ruin my evening with Tyrone. So I turned the radio up in the kitchen, and we bumped some

Erykah Badu as we made sure everything was perfect my man. Apparently, we were having too much fun and lost track of time because our concert was interrupted by the doorbell.

"Damn, time is flying. That has to be Tyrone. Cheyenne, get the door please! I need to go freshen up a bit," I said as I ran down the hallway towards my bedroom.

"Girl, what am I supposed to say to him?" she asked in a loud whisper.

"I don't know just ask him questions! I can't let him see me looking all raggedy," I replied as I slammed and locked my bedroom door.

Chapter 15

Cheyenne

I turned the music down a bit and made my way to the front door. *This is my chance to see if he's as great as he seems,* I thought as I looked out the curtains to see what type of car Tyrone was driving. At first glance, his truck looked identical to the truck Miguel was driving that night at the restaurant. However, I knew that couldn't be possible since Miguel lives miles away. I shook that thought off and opened to door to welcome Tyrone inside the house. When I opened the door, I was instantly blown away by the person waiting to enter.

"Um, Miguel? What are you doing here? How'd you find me?"

"Cheyenne? Uh... Hi..." he stammered.

"I didn't know you two knew each other," Marissa interrupted.

"Riss, this is Miguel, but I'm not sure how he got your address," I said.

"No, that's Tyrone. *My* Tyrone that I've been telling you about," she said.

We both looked at Tyrone, Miguel, or whoever he was, and he just stood there like a bump on a pickle.

"Miguel, aren't you going to say something? Is your name Tyrone? What are you doing here?"

I asked question after question without giving him any time to answer.

"Maybe I should just go," he finally said.

"No!" Marissa and I said at the same time.

"You have some explaining to do. I bought all this shit to give you a nice evening, and you have the nerve to think you're going to leave without explaining this fucked up situation to me!" Marissa yelled.

"Yea, and I'm still trying to figure out why my Miguel answers to Tyrone. What the fuck is up? After all the shit I told you about niggas and how much y'all are full of shit, and you still pulled a fucking stunt on me. I thought we had some real shit going, but I knew that wasn't so when your wife paid me a visit today," she spat.

"Wife?" I asked, feeling even more confused.

"Yes, his wife! I knew your ass was married!" Marissa said as she began to punch Tyrone anywhere her hits landed. "How could you do this to me? You're nothing but a two-timing, lying, mediocre sex, little dick ass bitch! How could you!?"

"Wait! I can explain! Just hear me out!" he said as he dodged her blows.

As much as I wanted to see Marissa continue to whoop his ass for both of us, I still wanted to hear what he could possibly have to say.

"Riss, chill! Let's hear this conniving motherfucker out."

"You better talk fast motherfucker, because I'm headed to get my little friend next," she said, referring to the .25 that she keeps in her purse.

We stepped aside and let him come into the living room. As he passed by us, he cut his eyes to make sure he wouldn't be met with more blows. Marissa and I sat on the sofa together, and he took a seat on the loveseat.

"Start by telling us your real name," I said.

"My name is Tyrone. I had no idea that you two even knew each other."

"Why did you tell me your name was Miguel?" I interrupted.

"Because it's my middle name," he said.

"So your name is Tyrone Miguel? You really expect me to believe that stupid shit?" I asked.

"Okay, you're right," he admitted. "Look, Miguel is the name I always use on those dating websites. I was going to tell you my real name if things seemed like they could grow between us. I never meant to hurt you," he said to me.

"What about me, motherfucker?" Marissa said angrily. "Did you plan to hurt me? Huh? And, what's up with you and your wife?"

"No, I never meant to hurt you either. And, well, my wife and I are separated. That's why I'm able to spend so much time with you. I didn't think it counted since we aren't together right now, that's why I didn't tell you about her," he said.

"I call bullshit," I said.

"He's definitely lying. He's not separated from his wife. They actually live in Chicago, and he's working on a contract here in town. She told me that he has an apartment here. I just can't seem to figure out how she ended up at our salon, though," Marissa added.

"Wow, so you've been lying to me this whole time?" I asked.

"I trusted you! After all the shit I've been through, I trusted you!" Marissa cried.

While I sat there trying to figure out how Tyrone's wife knew about us and the salon, Marissa began frantically shuffling through her purse. Tyrone obviously knew what she was looking for because he was halfway to his truck by the time the first bullet went flying through the air.

"Yea, you better run, you lying piece of shit!" she screamed as she continued to shoot at Tyrone's truck.

"Marissa! Calm down! You're going to get us both in trouble!" I said.

The sound of my voice interrupted her trance, and she abruptly stopped shooting. Her anger turned into tears, and she fell to her knees weeping. I didn't know if I should cry from pain or anger. I wanted to hold her and cry with her, but that would have been awkward since we'd be crying behind the same man. So I took the gun from her hands, placed it back in her purse, and went to the kitchen to turn off the food and the music. She no longer had a need for that.

Chapter 16
Tyrone

This has been one hell of a day. My cheating ways finally caught up with me and almost costed me my life. First, my wife pops in town unannounced and makes plans for us to be together. Then, she suddenly catches a virus and can't see or talk to me for twenty-four hours. Rather than push the issue, I made plans to see Marissa since it's been over a week since our last visit. However, those plans turned into my new chick answering the door at my girlfriend's house, and me running for my life as my girl unloads bullets at my ass. Luckily, she is a horrible shot, or else there would be some slow singing and flower bringing this Saturday with me as the main attraction.

On top of all that, Marissa tells me that my wife paid her a visit today. That could explain why she suddenly no longer wanted to spend the evening with me. What I don't understand is how she found them anyway. I'm usually very discreet with my shit, so I know I didn't slip up. I'll just have to feel with my wife out to see how much she knows. In fact, I need to give her a call just in case she's with my two side or ex-side bitches as we speak. I pressed her name on the touch screen system in my truck. As the phone rung through the speakers, I continued to think about everything that had just transpired. I mean, what were the odds of any of this shit playing out the way it did. Tosha has a hard time hiding her anger, so I'll be able to tell if something is wrong when I talk to her.

After a few rings, her voicemail picked up. I opted out of leaving a message and hung up instead. I continued to drive around for a while as I replayed today's events in my head. I knew I was wrong for dating friends, but it's really not my fault. Hell, I didn't even know they knew each other until it was too late. I was going to tell them when the time was right, but everything started moving so quickly in both relationships. Now, I have to figure out how to get back in good with both of them without getting myself killed. Until I figure that shit, I'm going to lay low from the construction site. I also need to figure out the real reason Tosha is in town. Something just doesn't feel right.

Chapter 17
The Queendom

When the group of wives and mistresses arrived at the queendom, they were impressed by the beautiful palace. The Queendom was a 20,000 square foot mansion on forty acres of land. The house appeared to be three stories tall, but the underground basement could not be seen from outside. The bright green grass stretched for miles and flowed with the hills of the land. There was a beautiful sculpture of Queen sitting on the throne dressed in Nubian attire. The sculpture was atop a beautiful fountain that glowed with a rainbow of neon colors at night. The long driveway was aligned with beautiful magnolia tree and rose bushes. Sexy men with sculpted bodies and gorgeous hues that ranged from dark chocolate to gold caramel worked the grounds. They served as yard men, pool cleaners, butlers, cooks, and anything else Queen instructed them to be. These men were either Queen's concubines or the exes of some of her clients. They were permanent residents of the Queendom, and they made no arguments about it.

As the ladies stepped out of the limousine that transported them from Vivian McQueen's office, they were greeted by a chocolate man with broad shoulders and a bald head. He was a mixture of Kem and Joe, and he had the brightest smile and most beautiful lips that the ladies had ever seen. Between looking at him and looking at the limo driver who had a dark caramel skin tone with juicy lips, deep dimples, and sexy dreadlocks with blonde tips, the ladies didn't know if they wanted to stay in the car or fall into the arms of the Joe lookalike. The aroma of YSL and the sexy tailored suit on "Joe" lured the ladies out of the car and toward the huge double doors that led to main entrance of the home.

The nine-foot tall Cherrywood doors added a Victorian appearance to the house. When the ladies entered the foyer, they were blown away by the beautiful crown molding that was engraved with various images of Nubian kings and queens. The shiny red and black marble floor contained specks of gold. The area was the size of an office, and everything was placed perfectly in its own spot. The scent of lavender gave a calming feeling as Kem's voice harmonized through the sound system of the Queendom. While the ladies oooed and aaahed at the beauty of the foyer, Queen seemed to appear out of nowhere. She was adorned in a long, form-fitting black dress that showed off her perfect sized breasts, nice hips, and round ass. Her hair was pulled back into an elegant bun.

She wore a black sequined mask that covered half of her face. Her eyes were familiar to the ladies, but they couldn't figure out her identity behind the mask. After standing and watching the ladies for a moment, Queen finally spoke in a bold yet sultry tone.

"Good afternoon, ladies. Welcome to the Queendom. Today, I will give you a tour of most of the areas of the Queendom. I advise you to pay close attention, because I will not repeat myself. When I am speaking, you are only listening. You are not allowed to ask me any questions, so I suggest that you get a partner and put your pea brains together. During your speaking period at the end of the tour, you will address me as Queen or Madam only. Should you decide to break any of the rules of the tour, be prepared to enter my quarters where I will punish you.

"You are here because you were not able to control your men just as your mothers weren't able to control your fathers. Some of your husbands cheated on you, some of your husbands physically abused you, and some of your boyfriends were married to some of the ladies in this group. As you know, Vivian McQueen's office conducted a full investigation on you and your mates. The wives were given an automatic pass to come here. However, the mistresses had to prove that they did not know the men were married. Mistresses, you are here because you deserve healing as well. Ladies, understand that your method of healing is up to you. As you read in the handbook that was provided to you at your last counseling session with Viv, you are responsible for getting your husband or *her* husband to come to the Queendom. I suggest that you refer to it as a retreat or resort instead of by the actual name.

"Sometimes things get a little dangerous here. For that reason, we have a medical team and a team of morticians on the premises. Hopefully, we won't need the latter, but shit happens. Unfortunately, the men that caused you so much pain don't always seem to find pleasure in the pain that is inflicted upon them. I see some of you are smiling and some of you of look like you've seen a ghost. For those of you that seem to be afraid, remember the contract you signed, and get over it. It is time for you to heal.

"There are four levels to the Queendom. The top floor is off limits without an invitation. The second floor is reserved for dinner parties and other events. Anyone who attends an event here is bound to a non-disclosure contract. At some point, you may see someone you know from your church, school, supermarket, law office, or wherever. My advice is that you focus on your own healing process and let them focus on theirs. The first floor is the spa area. This is where everyone relaxes and rejuvenates. There are three pools, two Jacuzzis, two saunas, a workout facility, a wine vault, and a cigar lounge on this floor. The chamber where all of the action takes place is located on the ground floor.

There is only one elevator that leads to that area. I will disclose the location of that elevator when you arrive for your first day of healing. There are six identical bathrooms on each floor, one kitchen on each floor, and many other rooms and bedrooms that you will see in due time. Here is one of the bathrooms."

Queen twisted the golden doorknob and entered the bathroom located at the end of the hallway. The ladies followed closely behind her. They were blown away by the beauty of the golden shower, faucets, toilet, bathtub, and shower head. The shower was large enough to hold at least ten people. There were ten shower heads. While the main faucet turned on the water, each shower head controlled its own temperature. The women whispered that they had never seen such an immaculate bathroom before. Queen let them take in the moment, and then she proceeded with the tour of the rest of the house.

The ladies followed closely behind her, and they hung onto every word she spoke. The nervousness of some of the women began to subside. They all seemed more eager to begin their sessions with Queen as they followed behind her like puppies. She continued to give them the house rules as she glanced at each of them periodically to check their demeanors. Queen wastes no time with fickle women. She expects them to have *some* strength after the sessions with Vivian. Any signs of weakness or indecisiveness will result in them being excused from the tour.

Chapter 18

Tosha

My meeting with Vivian McQueen was kind of different. She didn't say much, but she did something that was very questionable. It almost seemed as if she was coming on to me at some point, but I couldn't really tell if that was the case. I just know that she made me feel uncomfortable yet curious. After I gave her a briefing of what's been going on with my marriage, she asked me to cancel my plans for the evening to take a ride with her. I hesitated at first, but my curiosity made me do as she said.

When we got into her car, I almost changed my mind about going with her. She was a stranger that I had just met, and I didn't know why I was in her car or where we were even going. I just knew that I wanted to be in her presence for a while longer. I wanted to know more about her services and how she could help me regain control of my marriage. As we drove towards Highway One, I watched how Vivian caressed the steering so delicately. It was as if she was giving it a sensual massage. We didn't say much on the ride to wherever. We just kept making awkward eye contact and quickly glancing away.

After what seemed like a forty-five-minute drive, we approached a mansion that was surrounded by a humongous wroth iron fence. When we pulled up to the call box, Vivian entered a code, and the door of the gate began to open. She proceeded to pull forward.

"Is this your home?" I asked, wondering why we would be at her house.

"This is where your therapy sessions will take place should you decide to sign up for our services," she replied as she continued down the winding driveway that was lined with beautiful magnolia trees.

"Wow, this place is gorgeous. I'm sure it's very easy to find healing here," I said as I looked around and admired the beautiful landscaping and sexy men working in the yard.

Vivian must have noticed me drooling over the guys because she began to explain their positions to me.

"Those men are at the disposal of the Queendom," she began.

"Queendom?"

"Yes, this is the Queendom. Those men do what they are told to do at the Queendom. They work both inside and outside of the home until they are told to rest. If they lack in any way, they are punished," she said.

"Punished?"

"Yes, punished. Did you leave that non-disclosure agreement on Maria's desk?"

"Yes, I did. Why?"

"Great. You seem a bit uptight, so I want to be sure that you remember the terms of our preliminary agreement. I'd hate to have to loosen you up so soon," she said with a wink.

I quickly diverted my eyes and replied, "Yes, I remember everything."

Vivian pulled up in front of the house, and a couple of men appeared out of nowhere to open our doors. When we got out of the car, I followed her to the front door of the house. There must have been an automatic sensor on the door because it opened as soon as we walked up. An older gentleman that looked to be Jamaican greeted us as we entered to foyer. I nodded my head but never parted my lips as I continued to follow Vivian towards the back of the house. She led me to an elevator, and we took it to the ground floor. Once we were down there, we entered into a dark area that was illuminated by black lights and neon lights.

There were several hallways in this area, and there were lots of windows that showed the contents of the rooms. Each room had different items in them, but they all seemed to serve the same purpose. It looked as if we were in some sort of dominatrix torture chamber or something. Still, I didn't say a word as we walked through the area. I simply followed Vivian's lead. She finally spoke and broke the silence.

"So, what are you thinking?"

"I really don't know," I said. "I'm just observing. Wondering... Looking..."

"What are you wondering? Don't be afraid to ask questions."

"What is this place? On the outside, it looks like a nice mansion. Even the first level is beautiful. This area isn't ugly, but it's definitely different from the parts of the house I've seen. Is this some sort of torture chamber?" I asked.

"I wouldn't call it a torture chamber," she chuckled. "I'd say that it's more of our healing headquarters."

"Healing headquarters? Am I supposed to use these items to find healing?" I asked.

"Yes. Of course, you wouldn't be in the room alone. What kind of sick place do you think this is? Your husband will likely join you if you decide to hire us."

"Vivi..."

"Oh, that's another thing. When we're here, you will refer to me as Queen, Ma'am, or Madam. Failure to do so will result in punishment," she said without a cracking a smile.

There's that damn *punishment* word again. Either this bitch is crazy, or I'm crazy for coming here with her ass. I don't know where the hell we are, but some weird shit has to take place down here. Then, she's talking about me bringing my husband here. How the fuck does she propose I do that?

"Uh okay. So is this like some dominatrix shit or what? And, how do I get my husband to come here. I don't think he's into this kind of stuff. Hell, I'm not even into it."

"When you speak with him about it, you'll refer to it as a retreat. You may not be into it now, but after a few icebreaker exercises and a recap of your marriage, I'm sure you'll find a way to use the equipment for healing purposes. Do you have any other questions for me?"

"No, not at this time."

"Well, we can head on back to town. Hopefully, you'll be returning here within the next couple of weeks. I'll give you some time to decide," she said as we got back into her car and headed back to her office.

Once again, I rode in silence. I was trying to take in what I had just seen. I was also deciding if I was going through with her healing process or not. My curious side was really getting the best of me today. On top of that, Tyrone's cheating ways are getting out of hand. I just hope I make the right decision for the sake of my sanity.

Chapter 19

Marissa

A couple of weeks have passed since Tyrone got caught up. Cheyenne and I have continued business as usual, and we've avoided talking about the ordeal since it happened. We talked about it that evening, but we left it alone from there. Part of me thinks she's still talking to him, and the other part of me doesn't even care. I just know that I feel like such an idiot for the umpteenth time in my adult life, and I'm never dating again. I won't continue to subject myself to the bullshit and lies of these sorry ass men. If I didn't love dick so much, I'd even consider become a damn lesbian. Then again, women are crazy as fuck, too. I get on my own damn nerves sometimes, so I know another bitch would, too.

Tyrone has called me millions of times, and I've ignored and blocked each call. He even called from strange numbers, unknown numbers, and blocked numbers. Each time yielded the same result – blocked. There's nothing he can say to me. He played my best friend in the whole world and me at the same time. Plus, his ass is married just as I suspected. He's messed me up so badly that I don't even want to ride through downtown so I won't risk running into his ass. I even have a newfound hatred for asparagus, potatoes, and steak.

Oh, and I wrote a negative review on that organic food store. They didn't do anything to me, but that's where I got the food for my date with the liar. Therefore, they must suffer the results of that date as well. That damn pole has been snatched down and tucked away forever, too. I still have questions about this whole ordeal, but I don't want to give him the chance to lie to me again. I even wonder if Cheyenne knew and never said anything. My thoughts are all over the place, but I just keep busy to stop myself from drowning. So far, I've done well. I just need him to quit calling, and I need to trust Cheyenne again. I believe she's innocent, but I don't put shit past anyone. They say time heals all wounds. I guess I'm going to need a lifetime, because this pain is unreal. I really feel like I should get payback on him, and I think I know just who to call.

Chapter 20

Tosha

After visiting the Queendom with Vivian a couple of weeks ago, I'm convinced that I'm ready to find healing and peace with my marital issues. Tyrone has been surprisingly kind to me since my visit to Shreveport. It's like he's a new man or something. He's been home more often, and he even cooks and cleans around the house. It's like a switch flipped inside of him or something. Still, I'm going through with my plans to take him to the Queendom. I'm excited to see what all that place has to offer. Tyrone agreed to visit the resort with me, so Vivian has us scheduled to be there all of next week.

Although Vivian couldn't disclose much information to me, she did tell me that a scorned woman would be joining us at the retreat. At first, I was uneasy with that idea because I get this gay vibe from Vivian. However, I'm assuming it's the friend of the chick who did my nails. If she was also hurt by my husband, I guess she does deserve to find peace as well. Vivian assured me that she would let me call the shots though. Tyrone is my husband, and I have endured the most pain from him. The least I could receive is control of the revenge on him.

I'm really not sure what I hope to gain from this experience. Part of me wants to just let it go and forget everything I know about his infidelity. I just want to live my life as I have created in my mind – a nice home, loving husband, beautiful kids, and unlimited resources. Then, there's that part of me that knows I deserve better than to be cheated on and humiliated every day of my life. That part of me wants Tyrone to feel my pain in every way imaginable. That part of me wants him to suffer until he can't suffer anymore and he's begging to die. I want him to wish he no longer existed like I've wished so many times before. I want him to hate his life and the curse that has been on the relationships in his family. I want him to hurt, to cry, and to want to die. That's exactly what he'll feel in a few short days.

Chapter 21
Tyrone

I don't know what the fuck has gotten into Tosha's ass, but she has me at some weird ass sex place getting fucked up by some bitch in a costume. I can't see any parts of her face, and I don't know where the hell Tosha is. For all I know, it could be her crazy ass behind that mask. What I do know is that this has to be my last day living. With all the shit this crazy muthafucka is putting me through, I don't think I can last much longer. She has all sorts of jumper cables hooked up to my nipples and nuts, and she keeps sticking gay ass shit up my ass. Each time she does something to me, she keeps talking about the cheating I've done in the past.

Tosha told me we were going to a retreat, but I think we're at that place that the counselor sends women to all the time. All I know is one minute we were pulling up to a nice ass mansion in the country. We were greeted with fresh lemonade and cookies and shit. The next thing I know, I'm waking up in a dark ass room with my arms tied up and my legs spread eagle. There's even some weird music playing and people staring at me through windows all around this room. Some of the sick fucks are masturbating as they're staring into my eyes. Others are just staring, pointing, and laughing. It's like they find humor in my humiliation.

Each time I try to speak, the mystery woman smacks me with something. Sometimes her acts feel good; other times I regret the day I ever cheated on my wife. I've called out for Tosha several times, and she hasn't shown up yet. I keep asking this psycho who she is, but she hasn't uttered a word. I've tried to be still since it seems that my squirming fuels more rage. However, this bitch is not being gentle at all I don't know how much more I can take. Right now, I just want to go home.

Chapter 22
The Chamber

Tyrone hung naked with his arms stretched above his head and his wrists cuffed together. His legs were stretched apart, and his ankles were chained to two beams that were across from each other. His mouth was filled with a leather gag. Every time he tried to pull on the chains in an attempt to break free, his madam would strike him with a wooden paddle that had leather wrapped around it tightly. After every strike, Tyrone let out a moan that sent waves of lust through his madam's body. Watching his sexy, dark ass cheeks flex from the pain made Queen want to punish him even more for what he had done to his wife and the other two ladies. She wanted him to feel the pain that he caused those women when he used them as mere sex toys.

Madam would make him feel good by rubbing vigorously on his erect penis. Then, she would make him feel violated by lubing her fingers and milking his erection away. She could tell that he was exhausted from the whippings, erections, and milking. However, she had a duty to avenge the pain that he had caused so many women over the years. She wanted him to see what it felt like to experience pleasure that's quickly replaced with embarrassment and pain. The walls of the chamber were clear, which allowed others to view the concubine as he received his punishments. This was a pleasurable experience for some of the passersby. Loud moans echoed through the hallways as they pleasured themselves while watching the concubines suffer the consequences of hurting their women.

Tyrone was in for a long ride. His wife and his two mistresses were each going to have a turn with him over the next few days. Since he was so addicted to sex, Queen wanted to show him how bad overindulgence can be. He thought he had it made in the shade when he was running game on his wife and the other women. Madam was going to play a game of roulette with him. She started by clamping one testicle to each thigh. She also put duct tape in sporadic places on his hairy chest and abs. Tyrone's eyelids were pinned open to the point that he couldn't even blink, and his long dreads were tied around a spinning stripper pole. Each time Madam pressed the button on the remote, the pole would spin and wrap his hair more tightly around the pole, which pulled his head back even more.

There was an attachment that extended from the pole. It was positioned right above Tyrone's head and contained several eye droppers that were filled with hot sauce, bleach, salt water, soapy water, and acid. The roulette wheel listed different acts to be performed on the concubine. The acts ranged from eye drops to oral pleasure to electrocution and free spins. When Madam took the first spin, Tyrone's heart began to beat so rapidly that the heart monitor that was connected to him for safety began to beep loudly. This angered Madam.

"So, you're afraid of a little game of roulette, yet you played games with the hearts of three women?! You were such a macho man and playa playa when you thought you would get away with hurting your wife for the umpteenth time! You weren't afraid of putting your dick in so many women! Were you? Huh?! Oh, I forgot... You can't answer because of the balls in your mouth. You can't even nod your head for fear of being squirted in the eye either. Ha," Madam said with an angry, sarcastic chuckle. "Just relax. I may land on the spot that tells me to remove one of the torture items from you."

As the wheel spun around for what seemed like forever, Tyrone began to sweat profusely. The wheel began to slow down and looked like it would land on him receiving some head from Madam. His dick began to throb at the thought of her wet mouth on him. The wheel slowed more and more, and Tyrone thought he was in luck as it stopped on the spot he had hoped for. He smiled as his erect dick stood at attention and waited for Madam to please him. She walked over to him very slowly and sensually. She stood so close that his hardness pressed into her stomach. She slowly went down into a squatting position and retrieved a jar of honey from the supply table that was right next to where Tyrone was restrained.

Madam began to pour honey all over Tyrone's erection. As the honey dripped from his tip, she caught it on her tongue. He throbbed more and more as he anticipated her tongue. Before he knew anything, he felt strong, painful stings all over his no longer erect penis! There had been a few bees flying around in the honey jar, and they were now inflicting a pain like no other on Tyrone. Tyrone continued to moan and groan, and Madam just stood back and watched him suffer. She knew that the bees couldn't sting him more than once and that the pain would just be temporary. She was getting a kick out of seeing him whimper, whine, and beg for her help. While he ranted and raved, she relaxed with a glass of wine and thought about her torturing plans for later.

Chapter 23

Tosha

Being in control of Tyrone's feelings has given me some sort of renewed strength. I'm getting a real kick out of watching him squirm and beg for mercy. He finally even apologized for any pain that he has caused me. I don't know if he's being sincere or if he just wants me to call off the bees. Either way, it's the first apology I've gotten from him. All of the times he cheated on me, he's blamed it on the alcohol and swore he didn't know what he was doing. I pathetically believed him and continued my life as the wife that wasn't good enough to have a faithful husband. I always knew that I deserved better, but I allowed him to control me. Well, I'm in control today. I tell him when he can move, speak, cum, feel pain, or do anything.

"Are you tired of the pain yet?" I asked as I took over Queen's session with Tyrone.

"Yeah... Please stop," he said between breaths.

"Yeah? Did you say 'yeah' and fail to address me as Madam?"

"Madam... Please stop, Madam. I can't breathe. The bees... I'm... allergic... to the bees."

"And, I'm allergic to heartache and pain," I said as I watched him gasp for air.

I no longer felt a connection to him. I no longer cared about his pain. I only cared about making him feel what I feel. I couldn't breathe when I saw his emails with that Cheyenne bitch. I felt pain when I knew he was sleeping with the bitch down the street from us. Did he care about my pain? Did he have a desire to quit and let me catch my breath before he continued to hurt me? No! He just continued to cheat as I suffered through it all. Now is his time to suffer. Now is his time to feel pain.

Once he began to look lethargic, I decided to gather the bees back into the jar. As much as I wanted to hurt him more, I still couldn't bring myself to let him die. I pulled out an epi-pen and stabbed his thigh with it. Within in seconds, he seemed to be more alert. That only allowed me to take that bit of energy from him with my next act.

"Now that you've made a comeback, I'd like to welcome a couple of friends to the show," I said as I opened the door and let Cheyenne and Marissa enter the room. "You remember my nail technician, don't you? Maybe you know her business partner and best friend, Cheyenne. Seeing that you played them like you played me, I felt that it was only fair to let them have a turn with you. As your wife, I'm in control! These bitches will only do what I tell them to do to my husband. Now, Cheyenne..."

"Yes, Madam."

"I want you to choke my husband while you kiss him forcefully."

"Yes, Madam," she said as she walked over to Tyrone, removed the gag, and grabbed him by the neck. She began to kiss him softly as she gently gripped his neck.

"Cheyenne! I did not tell you to make love to my husband! I told you to choke that motherfucker while you kiss him vigorously! I know you're just a nail tech, but that means kiss the motherfucker hard and choke the shit out of him! Do I need to punish you?" I asked as I walked over and pushed her face into Tyrone's. "Kiss him! Bite him! Choke him! Have your way with him!"

"Yes, Madam," she said as she began to do as she was told.

Tyrone was still weak from the bee stings, so I knew he wasn't getting any enjoyment from it. Still, I watched Cheyenne make out with my husband. I figured it was time to turn things up a notch since he and every other man on earth likes the idea of a threesome.

"Marissa," I said as I walked over and gripped her ass.

"Yes, Madam?" she said uncomfortably.

"How many times did you fuck my husband?"

"I don't remember, Madam."

"You fucked him so many times that you lost count, huh?"

"I wouldn't say that."

"So you're calling me a liar?"

"No madam."

"So I'm telling the truth?" I asked as my grip tightened on her ass.

"Yes, madam. I lost count," she said and dropped her head in shame.

"Now is not the time to be embarrassed. Now is the time to face your shameful acts and find healing through my husband's submission. What was his favorite position with you?"

"He loved doggy style, Madam. He said that he loved looking at my ass."

"Ha! He told me the same thing each time we followed the exact same sex routine for sixteen years. We would start with him eating me. Then, he'd straddle my face and shove his dick down my throat for a few pumps. After that, he would pull me to the edge of the bed, spread my legs, and begin stroking me in and out for about a minute. Next, he would go down and eat me some more. I guess that was to stop him from cumming prematurely. Then, he would flip me over and moan and groan while hitting me from the back. Sometimes he'd oil my ass and rub it like a crystal ball. Other times, he's just slap it hard as fuck and grab my hair or my neck while he fucked me harder. Did he do that to you? Did my husband fuck you the same way?" I asked softly in her ear, letting my tongue graze her ear lobe.

"Yes, Madam," she said as she exhaled gently.

"Do I make you nervous, Marissa?"

"Uh... yes... um... no. No Madam."

"Make up your mind! Do I make you nervous, Marissa?!"

"No Madam."

"Do I seem mad, Marissa?"

"I wouldn't say 'mad' Madam."

"Well, what would you call it?" I asked.

"I'd say you're hurt or fed up with Tyrone's lies."

"You seem like a smart girl. I want you to do to my husband whatever he did to you. Did he fuck you doggy style?"

"Yes Madam."

"Fuck my husband doggy style," I said as I walked behind her and helped her strap on a big black dildo. "Cheyenne, that's enough. Let him come up for air. He'll need it for this next act."

While Marissa adjusted the strap-on, Cheyenne and I untied Tyrone and repositioned him on all fours on top of the velvet ottoman as he tried to resist us. He was still weak from the other acts, so it was easy for us to overpower him.

"Get on your knees!" I commanded.

"You're a crazy bitch! I'm not about to let her fuck me in my ass. Hell no!" he said as he continued to struggle with us.

"Get on your knees right now or I will cut your dick off! You made me crazy!" I said as I pulled a knife from the thigh holster attached to my costume. "And, you need to address me as Madam, or I will begin to cut your hair strand by strand. Do I make myself clear?"

"Yeah, whatever," he mumbled.

"I guess you think this is a game!" I said as I snatched one of his dreads and sliced it from his head. "Now, do you believe me?"

"Yes Madam! Shit!"

"That's more like it. Cheyenne, lube my husband's asshole please. I don't want Marissa to hurt him. Be sure to apply lube inside as well. It seems that Marissa has something really big and black waiting for him. It actually resembles the same dick we all shared. Well, Cheyenne, you didn't get your turn with him, but that's what it looks like," I said. "Loosen up, honey. If you just relax, it won't hurt as bad. Isn't that what you told me each time you wanted to have anal sex? Marissa, you may enter," I said and let out a loud laugh.

Marissa walked behind Tyrone and began to rub her dildo up and down his asshole just as he did me so many times before.

"Talk to him. Tell him the things he said to you, Marissa. I want to hear it. I need to know if my husband said the same things to you that he said to me. Talk to him while you fuck him," I said as I felt myself being turned on at the sight of Tyrone with another woman. "Cheyenne, let Tyrone nibble on your breasts to help him endure the pain that he's about to feel when Marissa thrusts her dick inside him. Marissa, fuck him!"

As Cheyenne positioned herself to allow Tyrone to use her breasts as comfort during his violation, Marissa shoved her dildo into his ass.

He let out a loud scream, and I laughed uncontrollably.

"Can't take it, huh? That's how I felt each time you insisted on me letting you explore your sexual fantasies. I don't know if anal hurt worse than the cheating, but they were definitely running neck and neck. Shut the fuck the up with that noise and take that dick! Marissa, let's give him some more lube," I said as I walked up behind her and began to rub lube all over her dildo.

I put more lube on my fingers and gently massaged inside his ass.

"Do you like that, honey? You seem to be loosening up," I said as I continued to massage him with Marissa standing between us. "You have all of us here together. Is this how you envisioned it, babe?"

"No... Fuck no!" he said.

"Are we forgetting something?"

"Madam! No Madam! This is not how I envisioned it. Look, I'm sorry. Okay? I've told you a million times! I'm sorry! Just get the fuck away from my ass, man. Damn!"

"Tell me how this makes you feel, Tyrone," I asked as Marissa resumed fucking him. "Do you like this? Does it hurt? Do you feel ashamed? How do you feel about these people watching you be humiliated by the person you vowed to love forever? It's not a good feeling is it!? Don't you want to die?! Don't you wish the pain would end?! You never thought I would do this to you, huh? Marissa, keep fucking my husband until I tell you to stop!" I said as I began to cry.

I needed Tyrone and so many other men to feel our pain. I wanted him to hurt like my mother, grandmother, aunts, sisters, and friends all hurt. Still, as much as I wanted revenge, I had to make it stop.

"That's enough! Get out! I don't want you near my husband ever again. Leave!" I yelled as I sat on the floor and cried.

Marissa and Cheyenne quickly left the room, and I untied Tyrone's wrists and ankles. I just couldn't continue to hurt him. Once again, he was in control.

Chapter 24

Marissa

Things continued to get weirder after the run-in with Tyrone. His wife invited me to dinner so we could talk. She even asked that Cheyenne join us. We agreed to meet with her because there was no way that she could kick both of our asses at the same time. While at dinner, she offered us some money to join her and her husband at a retreat. Cheyenne was game because it was going to be a free ride and she didn't care about Tyrone as much as I did. I gave it some thought and finally agreed to do it.

After getting the details of her plans, I was hesitant again. Then, she offered us five thousand dollars apiece to help her get revenge on her husband. She assured us that she didn't have plans to kill him and that we would actually find peace with our relationships with him. Since the shop still needed the renovations and we no longer had a guy to do it, we took the money and paid a different contractor.

When we got to the retreat, it turned out to be a dominance and submission place. Cheyenne and I wanted to make a run for it, but we signed a contract agreeing to submit to

Tosha's commands and remain quiet about the events that took place there.

I let her control me in the room, but what she didn't know is that I really wanted to take that dildo and shoved it down her throat for talking to me the way she did. She's acting like she was the only person hurt by her damn husband. Had she had better control of him, none of us would have been in that predicament in the first place. Cheyenne and I actually have plans for her since she wants to keep in touch. She made us do things that were far worse than what we did in college. That poor Tyrone is going to need some real therapy after what we did to him. That's what his *ass* gets – literally.

Chapter 25
Vivian

Watching Tosha crying uncontrollably after her session with Tyrone and his two women left me feeling dissatisfied. Usually, women find pleasure in getting revenge on their husbands, but Tosha was different. She truly loves him unconditionally. I can't say that she isn't crazy for almost killing him with the bees and the repeated pain that she inflicted on him, but I can say that she loves him. Thankfully, I never allowed myself to love any man like that. I was born with a hatred for them because of their evil, whorish ways. I've had my share of men, but there was never any real passion with them. I just needed them for sex, gifts, and money. I never loved any of them.

My mother loved my father, and that didn't stop him from raping her. My sisters loved their husbands, and that didn't stop the men from cheating or even making passes at women in the family. My friends loved their husbands, and that didn't stop the men from inboxing other women inappropriately. In my line of business, the therapy sessions usually work if the women really want to find healing. If the women are weak, they won't heal. They will end up like Tosha, feeling sorry for themselves and guilty for doing unto their husbands what they did unto them. Tosha's revenge acts likely got Tyrone's attention. He'll behave for a while, but I can guarantee he will revert to his old ways within two years.

She cried in front of him. That's where she fucked up. She let him see that she still cares. After all of the pre-counseling I gave her, she still showed him that she's weak. He knows that she will still love and protect him no matter what. She claims that she's with him for the kids, but their kids are older and know a broken marriage when they see one. What she's really doing is fucking those kids up and creating little Vivians and Queens. Maybe I should have assisted her with her full session, but she assured me that she could handle it. Maybe I should continue the counseling sessions with her and develop a closer, more intimate relationship with her. Then, I can encourage her to do things my way. Maybe I'll let Queen pay her a visit.

"Maria, contact Tosha Blackshire and tell her to come to the office. Cancel the rest of my appointments for the day. When she gets here, you are free to leave. I need to have a one-on-one session with her, and I don't need any interruptions."

"Will do," Maria said before she hung up.

Meanwhile, I turned on Whitney Houston's

Queen of the Night, closed my blinds, and waited for Queen's next concubine to arrive.

A READING GROUP GUIDE

Daddy Issues

Written by
Viv Love

About this Guide

The following questions are intended to
enhance your group's reading and
discussion of Viv Love's

Daddy Issues.

DISCUSSION QUESTIONS

1. Have you ever met a man like Tyrone?

2. Which of the ladies can you relate to the most?

3. What are your thoughts of Vivian?

4. Do you have an alter ego?

5. Did Marvin deserve what Shuntel did to him?

6. Do you think Tosha is weak?

7. What do you think of Cheyenne?

8. Do you think Marissa will continue to talk to Tyrone?

9. Do you think Tosha and Tyrone will remain married?

10. What do you think of the queendom?